D1061545

My Own Revolution

My Own Revolution

CAROLYN MARSDEN

CANDLEWICK PRESS

This is a work of fiction. Names, characters, places, and incidents are either
products of the author's imagination or, if real, are used fictitiously.

Copyright © 2012 by Carolyn Marsden

All rights reserved. No part of this book may be reproduced, transmitted, or stored in an information
retrieval system in any form or by any means, graphic, electronic, or mechanical, including
photocopying, taping, and recording, without prior written permission from the publisher.

First edition 2012

Library of Congress Cataloging-in-Publication Data is available.

Library of Congress Catalog Card Number pending

ISBN 978-0-7636-5395-8

12 13 14 15 16 17 BVG 10 9 8 7 6 5 4 3 2 1

Printed in Berryville, VA, U.S.A.

This book was typeset in Granjon.

Candlewick Press
99 Dover Street
Somerville, Massachusetts 02144

visit us at www.candlewick.com

R0427267821

For my family

CZECHOSLOVAKIA

The Downtrodden

Using my knuckles, I tap the pole. *Tappa-tap-tap.* The street sign jiggles. *Tappa-tap-tap.*

The guy will be tall, a beanpole like you, Patrik.

Tappa-tap-tap.

Overhead, the Communist banners flap their hammers and sickles in the breeze. The clock in the square says three minutes before noon. Three minutes left.

I look around. But casually. Not like it's any big deal. Not like I'm waiting for anyone.

The clock hand moves. Two minutes left. Small clouds run across the sky.

The others lean against the wall. Emil, his sandy hair cowlicked along the forehead; Karel, with his little, awkward shape; and Danika, who's wearing the bell-bottom pants she had to sew herself. Above them, the Czech and Russian flags fly side by side, bright against the gray buildings.

I, the tallest, was chosen.

This could turn bad. A person's doing a deal and a cop arrives instead. Or the other guy is really a cop. And thirteen-year-olds who make black-market deals? I don't want to know. *Tappa-tap-tap*.

I think of Adam Uherco, just a little older than us. Look at what happened to him. But, surely, buying off the black market isn't as bad as becoming a full-blown counterrevolutionary.

I hope not, anyway.

One minute.

A woman wearing a flowery hat passes. Not her. An old man struggles along with a cane. Not him, either. Five soldiers prance by, chatting and laughing. Definitely not them.

Maybe it's no one. No one is coming.

Emil's cousin lied.

Then a guy weaves in close. Tall, like Emil's cousin said. In a black leather jacket and black cap. Zero minutes. Our eyes meet.

He swerves, knocks into my shoulder. Says nothing.

I hand him the bills. He thrusts over a thin brown package.

Done. He's gone. Mingling in. We never met.

I wait by the pole, my hand sweating onto the wrapping paper.

After the clock hand moves twice more, I stroll over to the others.

"Make sure he gave you the right thing," says Emil. "Make sure you haven't been duped by a piece of cardboard. Make sure we didn't give over our allowances for nothing."

"Not here. We can't open it here. What if someone sees?"

Danika is leaning down, tugging on her bell-bottoms. As if she had nothing to do with this. As if she doesn't want this thing just as much as we do.

Karel whistles softly.

"Let's get out of here," I say.

Riding back on the bus, Danika refuses to sit with us. She sits up front, close to the driver. She's right to be freaked. What if a cop gets on? Could we make it out the back door? I will be the main one caught.

I feel through the wrapping paper. I find the hole, large enough for my thumb.

When we get to Emil's building, I'm not sure Danika will stick with us. But she does, mounting step after step. We're all a little breathless at the top.

Thankfully, Emil's parents are off working at their steel-mill jobs, and the place is wide-open free to us. His room smells like dirty laundry mixed with the smoke of the cigarettes he sneaks, but I'll get used to it.

"Now, give it to me," says Emil, reaching out. "After all, it was my cousin who arranged this."

We gather close and he peels off the brown paper. Inside, oh, yes, there's a record jacket with the Beatles' faces. Staring at us in black-and-white. And inside that, the shiny black disc.

"Hurray!" says Danika, giving one little clap. "Put it on, Emil. Let's listen."

Emil pops a plastic circle into the center hole so the single will fit the spindle. He flips the switch on the record player, and the light glows green. He turns the volume high.

The sound explodes out.

Of course we've heard this song before. Mostly on the radio, on the forbidden broadcast of the Voice of America. But now it's all ours. Here in Emil's room, we finally have it.

At the end of the song, the needle lifts itself up, moves back, then touches down again.

We lie on Emil's bed, listening and listening. The music is red and juicy with possibilities. It penetrates me everywhere. I want . . . I want . . . I want . . .

Pretty soon, a *knock-knock-knock* comes from underneath us.

"Damn," says Emil, lifting the needle. "It's Mrs. Zeman. She's beating her ceiling with a broomstick. Warning us to shut up."

We grow silent.

It's bad enough for this neighbor to complain about our noise. Much worse if she complains about our forbidden Western music. Black-market music.

"Couldn't we just listen quietly?" Danika asks.

Emil shakes his head. "Can't risk it."

Our fun is over.

Leaning up on one elbow, I page through a comic about Janosik. Janosik the legendary Slovak hero who stole from the rich and gave to the poor.

"You're way too old to be reading that," Danika says, lying back, teasing.

"Come on, Danika. How about the way Janosik defended the downtrodden?" Emil asks.

"And we're the downtrodden," I chip in. "We had to break the law just to get music."

"I didn't say that *Janosik* was babyish, only the comic."

"How can you not like this?" I open to a page, hold it up. "Janosik was resistant to arrows because of an herb he carried in his pocket. See—right here, the green flakes. He could move from place to place quicker than anyone else. *Whoosh!* And when he pressed his palm against a slab of stone, his hand left an impression."

"Mmm," Danika says.

The artist didn't do a great job of drawing the hand in the stone. In the margin, I sketch my own version.

"Hey!" Emil protests. "Don't vandalize my stuff!"

"You have to admit mine is better."

"A little," he says. Then he stares down at the floor, saying, "Damn Mrs. Zeman. She's probably phoning up some stupid party member right now. Saying that juvenile delinquents live upstairs from her."

"Even worse than juvenile delinquents," says Danika. "Counterrevolutionaries."

Karel raises a fist. Then he holds up the cover of the single, the Beatles' four faces staring back at us. "Wish I could at least have a copy of this."

I take up my East German EXA, which goes with me everywhere, and snap a photo. "I'll print this shot, and we can all have a copy."

"Better than nothing," says Karel.

With that, Emil slaps a whole stack of Janosik comics onto the bed. Each of us picks one, and even Danika starts reading about the adventures of the ancient Slovak hero.

The S and the R

In the shed out back of our apartment building, Danika and I search the shelves with a flashlight. The beam flicks. Here. There. But not on what we want. Old rags, old newspapers, garden tools. "Here we go," I whisper as the beam lands on a bucket of paintbrushes. I pick one out.

"And here," Danika says, guiding my wrist, aiming the light on the pots of paint.

I reach for the white.

"Oh, no," she says. "Green would look much worse."

"Yes, green. Too bad there's no pink. . . ." I hold open a paper bag, and Danika plunks in the brush and paint.

We head out of the shed, through the parking lot, lit with its pale, down-focused lights.

I clutch the bag to my chest, to where my heart is drumming. I'm like Janosik steeling himself for a raid. Janosik preparing to steal from the rich for the sake of the downtrodden. And Danika . . . Danika is . . . I can't think of whom to compare her to. Janosik had a sweetheart. At the thought of that word, my heart's steady drumming falters.

Danika and I have always been friends. As kids, we played Gypsies with a painted box. Danika wore her mother's skirts, Gypsy-long on her. We used brooms for horses. When the real Gypsy caravans came into our neighborhood, we spied on them. They threw back their heads and laughed, their gold teeth glinting in the light from their campfires. Their huge hoop earrings glinted. *Stolen gold,* one of us would whisper, and I shuddered at the thrill. Late into the night, I heard their wild music, music that didn't care who was in bed wanting to sleep. I knew the Gypsies were dancing, so lost in happiness that they forgot they lived in a gloomy Communist state.

Though Danika and I don't play Gypsy games anymore, we're still good friends. Just that. Not sweethearts.

Tonight we walk in and out of pools of light, under the looming trees. There are not a lot of ways we can strike back at all that pens us in. Things like Mrs. Zeman pounding on her ceiling. There's only little, stupid stuff.

Still, even the stupid stuff—getting away with stupid stuff—feels good.

We arrive at our big, blocky school, where the statue of the dictator Vladimir Lenin hovers over everyone. The building is pitch-dark. Even the janitors have gone home.

Long ago, the new moon set, leaving the whole night black. The distant streetlight barely illuminates the English words LONG LIVE THE USSR! The initials stand for the Union of Soviet Socialist Republics. They were painted last year when an important guy from England visited. Seeing that slogan, I've always imagined cleverly altering those initials. A simple change would do wonders. Now we're about to make that change.

I unscrew the lid of the paint. The night fills with a turpentiney smell, as if a whole forest has been squeezed into the pot.

Danika dips in the brush and stirs the paint, glancing over her shoulder.

I glance, too. Is someone lurking in the shadows? Could there really be someone? Is there really ever anyone?

After fifteen years of Communist rule, Adam Uherco's father escaped to America. He had to go, just couldn't stand this place anymore. Afterward, the party punished Adam's mother. Even though she was a lawyer, they sent her to do janitorial work at the car factory. Because she worked a long night shift, Adam hardly saw her. Even though he was a few years older than me — a stocky guy with close-cut hair — I remember Adam's anger well. I remember the way he painted anti-Soviet slogans on the school walls. He wouldn't stop, just wouldn't. In school he refused to wear his red scarf. He spoke out. He wouldn't stop speaking out. That is, until he got sent to the insane asylum.

And tonight I'm about to act like Adam. This could all go really wrong. But now that Adam's locked up, someone has to carry on. This is my own revolution.

"Let's do it," I urge Danika. "Get it over with."

Her hand shaking, she dabs out the S, dabs again, then gives the brush to me.

I look around once more. I check in with the drumbeat of my heart. All is well. With a quick swipe, I obliterate the R.

Danika giggles.

I stand back, the brush dripping. Now the slogan

11

reads: LONG LIVE THE US ! A big splotch of green replaces the missing letters.

All the closed gates open now. The fences fall. It's like stepping into a wide green field of freedom. It's like being Gypsies all over again. Squiggles of joy dance through me.

Stepping farther back, I aim my camera. I focus, holding steady, while the lens gathers the little bit of light.

"Let's *go*!" Danika says. "Someone's coming."

"Just a minute."

"I hear them—I hear footsteps."

But I keep calm until the flash bursts and the image is safely inside.

This time, we run, our own footsteps pounding into the night. The camera knocks against my chest, where those squiggles still dance. We've left behind the paint, the brush, and our shocking new slogan.

In the morning before school, a crowd mills around the wall. Danika and I pretend to stare like everyone else. Mr. Babicak, our principal, stands nearby, his arms folded, his thick glasses set firmly on his nose.

I glance down at my shoes. There is one tiny drop of green paint on the left toe. Damn. I should have worn the other pair. I sense Danika breathing beside me, giving off a scent of mint and flowery shampoo. I check to see that her shoes are clean.

Mr. Babicak is watching each boy's face. He thinks a girl would never do such a thing. He's looking for guilt. I try to look surprised. I try to look outraged.

Behind me, Karel and Emil giggle. One of them pokes me in the ribs.

Just as Miss Komar is writing an equation on the blackboard, someone clomps down the hallway. Pretty Miss Komar stops writing, her hand hovering, the chalk trembling ever so slightly.

Mr. Babicak enters the classroom. He stands for a moment, his eyes roving back and forth.

I slump down, push a pencil up the desk, let it roll back down. I push it . . .

At last Mr. Babicak says, "Comrades, my dear comrades, someone has betrayed the revolution." He pauses to let the words settle. I peek up to see his eyes landing on one face after another.

Miss Komar sits down behind her desk, sheltering behind a pile of books.

I wonder if Mr. Babicak has visited Danika's classroom. But then again, he's not looking for a girl. I stare at the kids in front of me, at the way the Young Pioneer scarves make neat red triangles down their backs. Like it or not, we all have to put up with being Young Pioneers.

I tuck my shoes under the chair. The spot of paint is so small. And yet it's the exact color. . . . Mr. Babicak's eyes meet mine. His stare lingers. I hold my eyes steady while my insides riot. For I am Janosik, eternally courageous, hero of the oppressed.

He comes over to my desk, looks under the chair.

Silence. A long moment.

Then he stands, points with his finger like the barrel of a tiny gun. "You," he says, pointing. "To my office."

As I walk down the hall behind Mr. Babicak, I try to guess where his invisible footprints are landing. I want to put my own feet exactly there. And only there.

Mr. Babicak slams the door and sits down at his desk. Behind him, the window glows with nice yellow springtime light. Yellow isn't right for my mood, but the window can't help it.

I take a seat in the straight-backed chair.

Mr. Babicak's thick glasses magnify his eyes. He says, "You have betrayed the people."

"Yes, sir," I say. When Janosik got caught robbing

the rich, he was chained to the wall of a dark cell to await trial.

Mr. Babicak touches his fingertips together, making a steeple with his hands.

I do the same with my own hands. Dust motes swirl in the light falling from the window.

Danika, it seems, will not be brought into this. Blessedly not.

"For the revolution to succeed, Patrik, all of us need to pull together. If one comrade pulls in the opposite direction"—he jerks his hands apart—"the chain breaks."

I hang my head. For all I know, I'll be demoted to a lower grade. I'll be sent away. I'll become the new Adam Uherco. Or maybe I'll only get suspended. If I get kicked out, at least I won't have to do schoolwork.

At least Danika has no paint on her shoes.

Mr. Babicak gets to his feet. Leaning on the knuckles of both hands, he hovers over me. "Just where do you and your family stand, Patrik?" He asks as if he's genuinely curious, but trouble creeps beneath the words.

The room grows still. Even the dust motes hang suspended. "We're strong party supporters, sir. I was just playing a prank."

Mr. Babicak sits back down. He swivels in his chair, twirling a fountain pen between his fingers. He pins me with his gaze.

I swallow hard. My parents are not party supporters. Not at all. Though only close friends know that about them.

"I certainly hope it was just a prank," Mr. Babicak says, then swivels some more.

"I will never do such a thing again, sir."

"I'm glad to hear that. Your punishment," Mr. Babicak says, tossing the pen onto the desk, where it clatters, then reaches a dead stop, "will be to stay after school for a week. Every day you will copy *The Communist Manifesto*. You will start tomorrow."

Janosik was tortured on the rack.

"Before you go home today," Mr. Babicak goes on, "come back to pick up a note to your father. You must return it with his signature."

Janosik was then hanged on the gallows.

Coming out of school, in the shadow of Lenin's statue, I whisper to Danika, "I got caught."

Her eyes widen. Eyes as blue as the sky behind them. "Now what?"

"Imprisonment. The Gulag."

"No . . ."

"Almost. Forced labor. Copying Karl Marx for five days."

"Oh, you poor thing."

The *S* and the *R* have both been painted back on, the wet paint shining, the oily smell stinking up the air. Hand drawn, the letters look clumsy.

"The slogan is so stupid now," Danika says, gazing away as if she has no interest.

In my bedroom, I slit open Mr. Babicak's letter to Tati. It explains that I vandalized a Communist Party slogan at school. That I am to be punished.

I want to hold a flame to this note. I want to burn it into just a black smudge. Instead, I uncap my fountain pen and forge my father's signature.

Chains

After school the next day, Mr. Babicak leads me to a small, dusty room off his office. On the desk lies *The Communist Manifesto*. He hands me a stack of lined newsprint and a fountain pen, then leaves, banging the door shut.

I pull out the wooden chair, clattering the legs loudly. Then I rock back and forth on the uneven legs. Outside, I can hear the shouts of kids playing soccer.

I uncap the fountain pen and draw a caricature of Mr. Babicak — beady eyes behind the thick glasses. The ink bleeds into the newsprint.

Opening *The Communist Manifesto,* I begin to copy:

The history of all hitherto existing society is the history of class struggles. Freeman and slave, patrician and plebeian, lord and serf, guild master and journeyman, in a word, oppressor and oppressed, stood in constant opposition to one another . . .

When Janosik died, they say that all nature went into mourning. The babbling brooks became silent, and the animals of the forest stilled in a sudden hush.

Out the window, I see the statue of Lenin. Underneath, a plaque reads: *Vladimir Lenin, 1870–1924, Leader of the October 1917 Revolution.* Every now and then, I look up and think of how Lenin symbolizes all that pins us down. How it's because of him that the heavy boots of the Communist Party trod upon us. Because of him that people like Mrs. Zeman can keep kids from having fun. Because of him that I'm copying this crap.

I daydream about pissing on him.

"Why are you so late?" Mami asks me. Her blond hair — with little strips of gray — is wound back in a bun. She's hung her nurse's cap on the peg but still wears the white uniform, the clunky white shoes. "You should have been home hours ago."

"I'm working on a project. With Mr. Noll. Doing a special report. I'm studying the ancient Greeks."

"Really?" She lifts her eyebrows.

I nod, then ask, "How was the clinic?"

Immediately, her eyes glow. "A baby came in very sick. But it was a simple matter of dehydration. With some proper fluids, that little thing was as good as new."

I match her smile. I feel bad about lying to her, but if I tell the truth about my punishment, she'll tell Tati. The two of them will start up the talk about getting out of here, of finding a way to escape Czechoslovakia.

I kind of like that talk. It sets me daydreaming about living in the West. Tati has an aunt in Pennsylvania who owns a gas station. When I was little, I thought Pennsylvania was *Transylvania,* home of Dracula. But it's a place in America. Whenever my parents daydream about escaping, it's always this aunt's gas station they talk about.

I daydream about wearing blue jeans and drinking Coca-Cola. If I were in America, I could play Beatles music all day long.

But my parents' escape talk is only frustrating. It never goes anywhere.

* * *

Each afternoon, I copy the *Manifesto.*

At the end of the day, I stand up and give the finger to Lenin.

Copying this crap makes me yearn to go to America. I'll even pump gas if I have to. In America people say whatever they want. They even talk bad about President Lyndon B. Johnson, and no one knocks them down for it.

On the last day, I come to the final words:

> *Let the ruling classes tremble at a Communist revolution. The proletarians have nothing to lose but their chains. They have a world to win. Workers of the world, unite!*

I lay down my pen, then pick it up again.

Because I'm pretty sure that Mr. Babicak will never read this, I change the words around: *Let Mr. Babicak tremble at the sight of me. . . .*

I carry the completed pages to his office. He's outside the door, locking up. As though he's planned to go away and leave me forgotten in the empty school.

When I hold out the stack of newsprint with its blots of ink, Mr. Babicak rifles through it. He hands it all back, saying, "I hope you've learned from this little exercise, Patrik."

"Yes, sir." I hold the paper close, as if it's precious. I hope my punishment has satisfied him. I hope that now he'll forget about me.

"You are dismissed," he says curtly. He says nothing about having a good evening.

There's a waste bin by the front door. I check to make sure that Babicak isn't around. Then, as though I am throwing a basketball through the hoop, I jump up and dump in my version of *The Communist Manifesto*.

Beef Stew with Turnips

"You two eat," Mami says, pacing. "I'll wait."

"Where is Tati?" my little sister, Bela, asks, and Mami swats at the air as if chasing away a fly.

Whenever our father is even a little bit late, Mami thinks he's been brought in for questioning, that he's losing his job, that he's being sent off to someplace where he'll never see his friends or family again. But usually he's late only because the bus is running behind.

We don't eat. Not even Bela. Mami opens the door, and we all listen. Maybe she's right. Maybe this time he's not coming. Bela grips Mami's hand.

At last we hear Tati's footsteps on the stairs. Two floors up he comes: 97, 98, 99 . . . And we thank our lucky stars that we don't live on the fourth floor, where

Danika lives, or the sixth or the ninth. The food would be stone cold by the time Tati got up.

Tati comes in and throws his briefcase on the coffee table. He squeezes up his face as he yanks his tie loose. My father's hair is receding, leaving a soft gray tuft in front. I touch my own hair. It's short but still nice and thick and growing all over. I don't ever want just that tuft on my head.

"What is it?" Mami asks, picking up the tie where it dropped. Tati doesn't usually throw his things around. "Sit down before you tell me," she says, pulling out his chair.

He doesn't sit, though. Instead he reaches into his pocket and pulls out a sheet of paper, saying, "Look at this." He places the paper in Mami's hand.

Reading, she narrows her eyes.

"Can I see, too?" I ask, leaning over Mami's shoulder. It's a letter headed with the government seal. Black words march across the paper, words about a man named Eduard Bagin. The words say that his diagnosis is mild schizophrenia and that the only work he is capable of performing is working on farm tractors.

"What does this mean?" I ask Tati, who is now shaking all over, his face as red as the Communist flag. But I don't really need to ask.

"It means . . ." he says. "It means . . ." But he can't go on.

Bela grabs him around the waist. *"Tati!"*

He puts one arm around her shoulders, but his eyes still dance wildly.

"What it means," says Mami slowly, "is that the party is ordering your father to diagnose this man as mentally ill. This poor man probably stood up for something he believed in. He was probably talking against the regime."

"And now he's going to the insane asylum, like Adam Uherco," I finish. As a psychiatrist, Tati visits the insane asylums. He says people scream and slobber, that they're tied up in nets.

"Not this time," says Mami. "This man will get a job he's too smart for."

"Mr. Bagin is a judge," says Tati, "at the downtown judicial building. I'm a psychiatrist, not their . . . their . . ." He pounds his forehead with the heel of his hand. "I refuse to play this game."

I take the letter from Mami and read it through again. It all sounds so logical, so matter of fact. I think of Mr. Babicak staring down at me, asking about my family. Could someone be forcing Tati to do this thing because I painted out a couple of letters on a wall? The smell of Mami's beef stew with turnips, my favorite, suddenly makes me queasy.

"Come eat," says Mami to Tati, this time pulling out a chair at the table. Steam rises from the soup pot, billowing into the dining room, into the light from the swinging lamp.

Bela sits down, and Mami ladles out a bowl of stew.

But Tati doesn't go to the table with the burgundy cloth, the cloth with the flowers faintly woven in. He plops down on the couch so hard that the cushions spring up. "I refuse to do it," he says. "I won't."

Mami crosses the room. She kneels beside the couch, taking one of Tati's hands in both of hers. "If you don't do this, what will become of you? Of us?"

I don't go to the table, either. Instead I open my history book and read: *Athens, the strongest city-state in Greece prior to the Peloponnesian War, was reduced to a state of near subjugation.*

Bela starts to cry, wiping her face with the edge of the burgundy tablecloth.

Tati buries his face in his big free hand. The clock ticks. The cuckoo bird slides out, pecking up and down. At last he says, "Okay, okay. I won't sign anything without at least seeing the man."

I flip the page and read: *Destroying whole cities, the Peloponnesian War marked the dramatic end to the golden age of Greece.* The black words swim. I memorize the words about the fall of the Greeks. The way they couldn't hold out. The way they just fell.

A Night Away

We travel with the windows of the baby-blue Fiat rolled down to let the springtime air in. Bela is sitting in the front on Mami's lap, dancing her doll up and down. The wind fills our hair with the smells of pine trees and fresh-cut hay. Danika sits next to me here in the backseat. Ever since we were little, she's always come with us to Dr. Machovik's vacation house in the spiky green pines.

This two-lane road winds through small towns, then through the collective farms, with their combines and tractors rolling through the fields. We pass a line of horse-drawn wagons. It feels good to get away from Trencin and Mr. Babicak and *The Communist Manifesto*. Away from whoever is bearing down on Tati.

In the front seat, Mami and Tati say things like "Look at that quaint house" or "Look at that new factory out here in the middle of nowhere."

The factory is called Eastern Slovakian Steelworks. Under a hammer and sickle, two painted slogans scream at passersby: *Long Live Communism!* and *By working hard, we'll have success in our future!*

Tati snorts. "No one wants to work hard. If you do, there's no reward. If you slack off, there's no punishment."

If we ever get to America, I'll work hard pumping gas at my great-aunt's gas station.

"Look at that," Tati says, braking and pointing to a policeman with a radio. "See him talking into that? He's informing his buddy on the other end of the village that we're coming through. If we arrive too soon, we'll get a speeding ticket."

He pulls up to a small shop. First he takes his time wiping down the windshield, then he goes inside. After a while, he comes back out carrying a small box of chocolates, saying, "No speed trap is going to catch us! The government isn't going to get extra money out of me!"

Mami opens the box, gives a chocolate to Bela, then gives it to me. Danika and I each unwrap a chocolate, the gooey sweetness melting onto our fingers.

Danika rests her arms on her violin case. She takes that violin everywhere. As we drive, she hums bits of the Vivaldi piece she's working on.

We arrive at my favorite part of the trip: passing through the Tatra Mountains with pines piercing the sky and the pointy snowcapped peaks. If you ride the ski lifts, you can see all the way to Poland. Here in the Tatras, Janosik and his band of loyal men hid in tough times.

Tati stops and we get out and stand shivering, gazing at the glaciers. I find myself wondering what kinds of mountains they have in America. I lift my camera and capture the folds and flow of the largest peak.

Danika moves closer. As her shoulder brushes mine, I wonder if Janosik's sweetheart also hid out in the Tatras.

Since the light is falling in the valley below, we climb back into the car for the last part of the trip. We cruise out of the mountains, back to the villages and collective farms.

At last we arrive in Shindliar, a little town lined with brick houses enclosed by white picket fences. Tati turns down a dirt road into the pines. The rutty road jostles me against Danika until we pull up at a house with a steep-pitched roof covered by emerald-green moss. Smoke unfurls from the chimney.

Dr. and Mrs. Machovik come out the front door, the doctor with his pointy goatee, and Mrs. Machovik wiping her hands on her apron. Dr. Machovik has been our family doctor since I was born.

They stand waving while Tati parks the blue Fiat. When we get out, they gush on about how Bela and Danika and I have grown. The collie, named Tulo, licks and jumps against my legs. I settle him down, pressing my cheek into his fur.

Dr. Machovik takes us around the side of his house to show off his garden of tomatoes, squash, and peas. He shows us the currants Mrs. Machovik makes into jam. He explains that when he's in Trencin being a doctor, the neighbor cares for all of this.

"I'm lucky the government lets me grow anything at all. They want everything collectivized." Dr. Machovik bends down to yank out a weed. "But without these little gardens, we'd all starve. I should give half to the government, of course," he says. "Instead I give to my friends and declare less."

Danika and I make faces at each other. We've heard this rant before.

With a smile, Mrs. Machovik takes Bela's hand and

leads her away to the crisp blades of new tulips bursting through the soil.

Meanwhile, Dr. Machovik starts showing off the white boxes housing the bees. I used to be afraid of bees and hid in the house whenever Dr. Machovik put on his bee suit. But today only a few stray ones wander through the early-evening air. "In the winter I feed them sugar," Dr. Machovik says. "That makes inferior honey." He chuckles. "That's the honey I give the government." He chuckles again.

I know where this conversation is headed. Dr. Machovik and Tati will rage over the way the Moscow advisers are handing down unworkable policies for Czechoslovakia. *Willy-nilly,* they'll say.

"Let's go to the river," I say to Danika.

The springtime river, which has angled down from the Tatra Mountains above, is a leady color with sharp whitecaps. In the summer, it'll turn green and lazy again, glinting with yellow sparkles. We'll picnic and sunbathe on the hot sand, then jump into the current, which carries us to the river's bend. Just before the white water, we'll climb back out and return by the forest trail.

The light dims, and the river becomes a blur. The pines turn gray. The voices of Tati and the doctor grow softer as they retreat into the house. Finally, Mrs. Machovik calls us to dinner.

Inside the house, good cooking smells fill the air. I take in the familiar shelves of porcelain figurines, the photographs in their silver filigree frames. There's even one of me and Danika playing with a ball. Lace doilies extend over the arms of the chairs, the back of the sofa — everything crocheted by Mrs. Machovik.

"Come here," Mrs. Machovik beckons. She lifts the lid of a basket. Inside, nestled in flannel, lie two newborn bunnies, their eyes still closed.

"Their mother was killed by a cat," Mrs. Machovik says, handing one bunny to Bela, another to Danika, "so I took them in." Danika's bunny opens its tiny pink mouth and yawns.

I reach out a fingertip to caress the little head. But I find it's not the rabbit I care about. Suddenly I want to stand right next to Danika, just as we stood at the river. That word *sweetheart* bounces into my mind, but I bounce it right back out. Danika and I are like sister and brother. Simply that.

"And now, back into the basket," says Mrs. Machovik, lifting the lid to the bunnies' bed. "Dinner's ready."

Shivers

We sit down to potato dumplings and tiny lettuce leaves just picked from the garden. For dessert Mrs. Machovik serves fat red plums the neighbor canned.

"We trade our produce," says Dr. Machovik, winking.

After dinner, when the house is lit by soft yellow lights, Tati and Dr. Machovik sip coffees spiked with splashes of brandy. Outside, the crickets are starting up.

Mami helps Mrs. Machovik with the dishes in the kitchen big enough for only two, while Bela cradles her doll and watches the bunnies sleep.

I reach for two packs of cards on the sideboard and hand one to Danika. We start up a game of double solitaire, laying down our cards with precise little clicks.

Tati turns the conversation to the reports of race riots in America. Negro people are said to be fighting with white people. In their battle for equal rights, they're led by a fiery preacher named Dr. Martin Luther King.

Humming under her breath, Danika lays down three cards in a row, then draws three more.

"Such a thing could not happen in that great country," claims Dr. Machovik, lighting a cigar. "It is all propaganda by our own government to discredit the great U.S. of A. Like the way they say people have to sleep under bridges. How in such a wealthy country could that be?"

"Americans couldn't possibly be treating those dark people badly," says Tati. "America is the land of the free."

"They did have slavery," I say. I know this fact from my history books, though I know nothing for myself about Negroes, never even having seen one. I lay a black ten on a red jack.

Dr. Machovik waves my words away. "Slavery was a long time ago. Every country has its less admirable moments." His voice floats into the golden glow of the living room.

"I saw a newsreel about the race riots," I can't help but say. "I saw Negroes being blasted with water hoses, being attacked by German shepherds. How can the Soviets fake that?"

"Huh." Dr. Machovik chuckles. "The Soviets are very clever."

Maybe he's right. Surely Tati's aunt would have said something if there were race riots going on in Pennsylvania.

"For the purposes of propaganda, anything can be fabricated," Dr. Machovik states. "Even newsreels." He pounds his fist lightly on the arm of the chair.

Tati and Dr. Machovik light their pipes, fruity smoke curling out. Tati leans close and begins to tell about what happened with Eduard Bagin. About how from out of the blue, orders came to demote this man to tractor driver.

I flip through all my cards. Nothing to play. Suddenly I'm stuck. I wait for Danika. But she's got nothing, too.

"Never have I had trouble like this before," Tati is saying.

Dr. Machovik strokes his goatee.

With a loud slap, I throw down my cards, hoping to distract Tati. He shouldn't be telling this secret story. Not even with this man who has been our friend for years and years.

"I've always been left to do my job as I see fit," Tati goes on.

"Let's go outside," I say to Danika.

We slip away to sit on the porch steps. Tall pines poke like leafy spires into the night, and the first stars have appeared. Tulo circles three times, then lies at our feet.

"Remember how we used to play hide-and-go-seek in those bushes over there?" Danika says.

"And how we played badminton without a net."

"And you cheated, always sending me the birdie so low." Bare armed, Danika suddenly shivers.

Her shivers pulse into the night, pulse against my skin. Feelings get jolted loose. Feelings I didn't know I had.

"Here," I say, taking off my jacket. But instead of handing it over, I tuck the jacket around her shoulders. Suddenly I don't feel merely brotherly. My arms linger. They don't want to pull back. They want to *enfold* her in the jacket.

But I've never touched a girl like that before. Never wanted to. I draw away and press my legs tight. Without my jacket, I'm the one shivering.

Hell's Bells

If we can't see the Beatles, at least we can be them. With the record player turned low for Mrs. Zeman's sake, we line up in a little group by Emil's closet. Karel, shorter than any of us, beats a pot while Emil and Danika take turns pretending to strum an old guitar. I'm technically the singer, holding a can of green beans for a microphone, but we all sing along at the good parts.

Emil, who never dresses up, wears his Sunday jacket, trying to look like John Lennon. He's punched the lenses out of an old pair of glasses and wears the empty frames.

In spite of her short hair, Danika looks nothing like a Beatle, nothing like a boy. Since Shindliar, the feeling of just being friends has vanished. Every word is loaded with meaning. Each tiny glance sets my body humming.

The songs themselves set me humming. They get inside me and tear apart all I ever was. They break me free.

Soft as the music is, Mrs. Zeman's broom handle starts rapping against the floorboards.

"Hell's bells," says Emil. "What a toad."

"It's all the fault of the stupid party," Karel says. "If it wasn't for the party, we could play all the music we wanted." Karel has only started caring about music. Up until recently, he's spent his whole life with model trains, the tracks winding over his bedroom floor. But now he wants to listen to the Beatles all the time.

"We could buy whatever we wanted," I add. "We wouldn't have to *share* photos of the record jacket. We could each have our own." Saying this, I realize I still haven't printed the promised copies.

"The kids of those party members have everything," Emil says. "Their parents drive fancy Russian Volga cars."

"The mothers wear diamonds like ice cubes," says Karel.

"They don't care about the proletariat breaking loose from their chains," I add.

We're shouting now, trying to outdo one another. We're even louder than the music Mrs. Zeman pounded her broomstick about.

"They don't care about the fall of the ruling class."

"They want to *be* the ruling class."

"The party goes on and on about how Western music undermines the family," Karel says, "but their own kids listen anyway."

"They're all undermined," I add.

Only Danika has said nothing. Sitting on the edge of Emil's bed, she's grown quiet. She picks up a candy bar wrapper from the floor and folds it smaller and smaller.

"Stupid party." Karel punches the air.

"Hypocrites," Emil adds.

"Someone is always trodding us down," I say.

Suddenly, Danika throws aside the candy wrapper. It lands on the floor, springing loose from the tight folds. Then, her lower lip trembling, she says, "It's not *trodding*. It's *treading*. *Treading* us down. *Trodding* isn't even a word."

"So?" asks Emil.

"It should be right."

Karel laughs awkwardly.

Emil and I exchange glances.

I reach over and lay a hand on Danika's shoulder. "What is it?" The words *my darling* spring to mind. I want to add those two lovely words but don't dare.

"It's nothing. Nothing to do with you." She shrugs off my hand.

"Something to do with the Beatles?" She could be hopelessly in love, as so many girls are.

She shakes her head, her short hair wisping out.

"Sure you don't have a crush on Paul McCartney?" I say lightly, trying to make a joke.

She shakes her head again, harder.

If only she were cold, I could offer my jacket again. This time I'd be brave. I'd put my arms around her pretty shoulders, driving away her troubles. At the thought, my heart does a quick somersault.

Emil goes very quietly to the record player. He lifts off the single and slips it into the jacket.

Karel picks up the old guitar and begins to pluck the strings.

Danika turns to him, saying, "Don't do that. Just don't."

"Danika." I get up from my chair and lower myself onto the bed, sitting next to her. She's pale, and her

blue eyes are moist. Maybe it's her monthly time. I consider drawing her close, even without the excuse of the jacket.

But she abruptly tilts away from me and flings herself down on the bed. "It's no use," she says. "This isn't something you can fix, Patrik."

The Bratislava Boy

In the school gymnasium, we're marching with our knees high, our hands behind our backs. Suddenly, as we're drilling to make us better Young Pioneers, training to take on challengers of the Communist state, there's a stranger among us. His curly hair covers his ears. Like a Beatle. Like the way I sometimes imagine my own hair. I run my hand over my close-trimmed head. "Who's that?" I ask Karel without moving my lips.

"Bozek Estochin. From Bratislava."

Bratislava is the big city where anything can happen. Whereas Trencin is like the tiny moon of some far-out planet like Neptune, Bratislava is like the sun. Someone new and exotic has landed in our midst.

* * *

After school, Bozek comes down the steps while Karel is bragging about how we got our Beatles single on the black market. Bozek doesn't walk like he's the new kid. He's not shy at all. His legs move loose and jaunty as he comes to us, saying, "I have that single. And I have 'Please Mr. Postman.' I even have a Monkees album."

We shut up and look hard at this guy.

"I even know where in Bratislava people can get real American blue jeans," he says. "The price is high, of course. The lines are long. But you can get them."

Emil squints.

I squint, too. What kind of life does this city boy lead?

Karel leans against the railing, frowning. Maybe he's thinking that Bozek could get him the model-train parts he can't find in Trencin.

Even though people are trying to get by, Bozek stands with his hands in his pockets, his elbows jutting out, taking up space. "In Bratislava, I listened to three Beatles songs in a row. Just waiting around outside a Bratislava apartment window I heard that."

I shade my eyes to better see this guy. Maybe he's for real. Or maybe he's only bragging.

Bozek glances around. "The girls in Bratislava even wear miniskirts. Of course there would be none of that here," he says. "Nothing like that here in an out-of-the-way place like Trencin."

"Then why did you come here?" I can't help but ask.

He shrugs, says from the corner of his mouth, "It's just for a little while."

"How long?" Emil asks. Maybe he wants another Beatles single. Maybe a whole album.

"As long as my father is assigned here."

"And what does your father do?" I ask.

"Can't say." Bozek lifts his eyes to Lenin's statue.

Can't say means he's a party member. His father is one of the boots that trods on us. Treads on us. I tread down a step, backing away.

Behind Bozek, along the wall, the repaired slogan blares: LONG LIVE THE USSR!

A group of girls has gathered at the bottom of the stairs, huddling and giggling. Over the tops of the piles of books in their arms, they peer up at the new boy. One of the girls is Danika. She's staring at Bozek as if he's dropped from the heavens.

Danika, my very own Gypsy. My sweetheart.

Bozek pauses in his storytelling. His eyes shift to the girls. His eyes glide over them. Will he really care about Trencin girls when the ones in Bratislava are wearing miniskirts? He settles on one girl.

He raises his hand, as if about to wave at her.

She blushes.

What the hell is going on?

And then, in a flash, my whole world changes. I look at Danika and see Janosik's lovely sweetheart. Or a Beatle's girlfriend. I see a beautiful girl who could be, should be, my girlfriend.

I step back onto the next step, level with Bozek. "Stay away from her," I say quietly.

"Oh, really," he says, not seeming to care that I tower over him.

Now he's more interested than ever.

I drop my books and grab the red Young Pioneer scarf around his neck.

Karel pries my fingers loose. "Don't, Patrik."

"You don't want to get in trouble," Emil says.

Karel takes me by the forearm. Even though I loom over him, he leads me away. Emil gathers my books off the steps.

Everyone is staring. "Let me go."

"Not yet," says Karel.

Not until we get to the street does he release me.

When I look back, Bozek is moving down the steps toward Danika.

"You can't do anything about it, Patrik. Nothing," says Karel. "Don't make an idiot of yourself."

"Forget her," says Emil. "There are plenty of other girls."

Not like her, I want to shout. But I force myself to look away, saying, "Okay, okay. But leave me alone now. I promise I won't go back. I won't."

Wandering into a clump of trees, I sit down with my back against the trunk.

My friends stand around.

"You don't have to babysit me."

"Then don't do anything stupid," says Emil. "Promise?"

"Promise."

And then they're off and I'm left with a pile of chewing-gum wrappers and old beer bottles. Behind me, Bozek, the son of a party member, is moving in on Danika.

I take off my red Young Pioneer scarf and knot and unknot it. Any minute now, Danika will pass by here. When she does, I'll step out and walk her home.

But she doesn't come. I wait for her until the tree shadows grow heavy.

Has she—? The thought makes my stomach flip. Has she gone off with Bozek?

Rotten to the Core

I have to find her. I check out hiding places in the lanes, behind bushes. A place where a boy could pull in a girl for a quick kiss. But there's nobody.

I go back to our building and up the 115 steps to our apartment to lie in wait.

I position myself at the open window, my heart doing cartwheels.

Sure enough, when she comes, she's with him. They come up the walk together. My heart twists. I peer out, but keep hidden. She mustn't think I'm spying on her.

She and Bozek are standing close. The schoolbooks in their arms almost touch. They're both still wearing their red scarves. They're still wearing those even though it's after school and they no longer have to demonstrate party loyalty.

They're idling on the walk, which is edged with flowers that Mrs. Smutny planted, kneeling in those cold fall days, pressing bulbs into the soil with her arthritic fingers. They're looking into each other's eyes right where Danika and I have played jump rope and hopscotch.

I lift my camera over the windowsill and, without sighting, snap a photo of her. At the last second, before I can lift my finger, Bozek moves into the frame. Now I have mistakenly photographed not just Danika, but Danika and Bozek.

"Patrik!" Mami calls. "Come for supper."

"In a minute," I call back. "I'm finishing some homework."

I can't leave while Danika is down there. I have to know what happens. I can't just leave these two unobserved. Maybe she'll come up when the light falls. And Bozek will go away. Far away to wherever he lives. And then I can eat.

At last he leans a little closer. The books touch. Is she holding hers like a barrier? Or does she tilt them just to the side so that Bozek can edge closer? I lean farther out.

Too far. Danika looks up, sees me, waves. She calls out, "I see you up there, Patrik!"

But she doesn't guiltily draw back from him. She doesn't think I care.

Shielding his eyes with one hand, Bozek looks up, too. He waves as well. I wave back. But I'm not waving to him.

Finally they whisper something together, laugh together, and Bozek goes off down the walk, looking back once, then again. I hear the big door of our building slam. Danika is inside at last.

I go out and race down the stairs.

Coming up, she's a little breathless, her short hair ruffled. I want to toss aside her books and tell her everything.

But she speaks first, her cheeks flushing. "I saw you take a picture of us, Patrik. Can you develop that photo tonight? I want to show my friends."

I stare at her. And stare some more. How could she ask such a thing? How could she *dream* of asking?

"You don't have to blow it up big," she goes on. "Small is fine."

"Not tonight," I tell her. "There's too much film left on the roll."

I turn up the stairs, away from her. I fly up the stairs and into our apartment.

Mami has put on the burgundy cloth and the lace

place mats under the plates. Bela is already sitting at the round table, eating applesauce alone instead of with her pork chop. She spoons it in, and it runs down the sides of her mouth.

Danika is probably at the door to her apartment. She is fitting the key into the lock since no one is home. I should go on up. I should apologize.

Mami goes to the window and looks out at the path that Bozek just walked down. Bozek, going away. She's waiting to see Tati walk up it.

I take a pork chop and dollop on some applesauce. I fork a pile of sauerkraut onto my plate, and then Mami cries out and hurries to the front door.

Instead of using my knife and fork, I pick up the pork chop and take a bite.

"*Patrik!*" Bela says, and I stick out my tongue at her.

"Yuck," she says, "your mouth has chewed-up pork chop inside."

I laugh, teasing her.

Tati comes up the stairs. He comes inside but doesn't greet any of us. He sits and rubs the back of his neck with one hand. "Jakub Machovik has joined the party," he says.

Mami's eyes grow wide. "No!" she exclaims.

"Yes," Tati says simply.

"I can't believe it."

I too think Tati must be joking. How could our family doctor have done such a thing? Not long ago, we were all together at his vacation house in the pines. And Tati was even telling him about Mr. Bagin. . . . My mind flits away from that terrible thought. Instead I wonder if now Mr. Machovik will report all his vegetables and honey and give half to the government.

He won't. All party guys get rotten to the core. Even I know that. The party is like a worm working its way into a crisp red apple. It gets at your soul. I wonder what's become of the newborn bunnies.

"How did you learn this news?" asks Mami.

"It's official. He's closed his office and moved downtown." Tati glances at Bela, who is scraping up the last of her applesauce, then goes on: "He's evidently in a position of power. Probably because they snared a doctor they did that for him right away. Word has it that he's demoted Dr. Csider. For the way he joked about how the building materials for the new post office got carted away and sold on the black market."

"What's happened to Dr. Csider?" I ask, Mami's food now funny in my stomach.

Tati spears a pork chop and lands it on his plate with a little thud. "Dr. Csider," he says, "is no longer working as a doctor. He's been sent to do roadwork way up by Prikra."

Mami gasps, and Bela looks at her sharply.

Everyone is getting demoted these days. Lawyers become window washers. Teachers go to factories. And Adam Uherco, a kid just like me, is locked up.

But I can hardly imagine Dr. Machovik making skinny old Dr. Csider work with asphalt. Just for cracking a joke.

Will something now happen to *Tati*?

Will something happen to all of us?

"Why would Dr. Machovik join up?" I ask.

Tati shrugs. "For the money."

"But he's a doctor," Mami says. "Surely he's got a decent income."

"For the power, then. For even more income."

A cold shadow falls across us.

"But a little while ago, he was on our side," I say. "He was bragging about how he cheats the government."

"Becoming a party member doesn't mean he likes the government any better than he did before." Tati cuts the pork chop off the bone. "He just sees an opportunity to use that government."

"Against us?"

"Let's hope not."

I finish eating and rinse my plate. "More home-work," I say, excusing myself. I go to my room and into the closet, which is my darkroom.

I shut the door, and the room goes black. I can't stand having a picture of Bozek with Danika in my camera. Even though the film isn't completely used and film is sometimes hard to get, I take it out and roll it onto the reel.

I plunge the reel into the baths and go to work. At the end, I turn on the red light and look at the strip of negatives. Only the last shot is important. It shows Danika and Bozek on the walkway, leaning close with their books almost touching. Even though the nega-tives aren't completely dry, I make a print of the shot. Before the paper even dries, I take a pair of scissors and cut Bozek out of the shot. I cut him away from her so that she is separate from him. I hang the image of just her on the inside of the door, then hesitate over Bozek's image. I could burn it. Or cut it into a million pieces. But I just drop his face—smiling over his red scarf, which is just dark gray now—into the wastebasket.

Danika lives two floors up in an identical apartment. Years ago we lined up our beds so hers was right on top of mine. At this moment, she may be exactly above me. Is she lying up there daydreaming of Bozek?

When we were little, Danika and I started the note dropping, and we've kept it up all these years. She lowers a note on a string until it dangles where I can see it. She used to tell me how her teddy bear lost its button eye or ask things like what Mami made for dessert. Now she tells me different things. She tells me when she's had a fight with her friend, asks my advice on how to make up. After I read her note, I always scribble a response. When I yank on the string, she pulls the message to her window.

Because she lives above, Danika has to be the one to start. Now I wish she'd send a note down. Say something. I'd answer right away. I'd send her a sweet note. I'd apologize. She'd sweetly accept.

And then I'd send her another message with three simple words.

Walking to School with a Violin

I wait for Danika as usual on the walkway. But this morning I combed my hair and pressed my shirt. I shined my shoes until I could see my face in them, so distorted I looked ugly and thought: how would she ever love me back? I'm even wearing my stupid red scarf because I think she must like it.

Danika is late this morning, so I pace the walkway. I see a pink flower with a yellow heart and think I should pick it for her and spill out the words that go with it. But I'm not ready yet. Not now that we are late.

She comes out the door, letting it bang shut behind her. Her hair falls carelessly over her forehead. She's carrying her violin case, and I remember that today after school she has her lesson.

"Let's go," I say, but she's rustling in her bag. She's off-kilter and distracted.

I offer to carry her violin case.

She looks at me funny, since I've never offered before. "Why, thank you, Patrik."

We walk to school with the lilacs blooming, birds nesting in the trees. We walk over a fallen nest with tiny crushed blue eggs.

We arrive at the blocky building, the looming trees, our vandalized slogan, so sloppily repaired. The statue of Lenin lifts an arm as if to say, *Here I am, ruler over all of you.* Once he may have been famous for fighting for the downtrodden, but now he's the one doing the trodding. I mean treading. He's a giant stomping boot.

I follow Danika through the big door, and then she is gone. She's lost to me in the sea of red scarves. She goes so quickly that she forgets her violin.

I leave the violin in the office. I write a note, then hesitate before signing my name. Should I draw a heart? That would be a girlish thing to do. The secretary is already holding out her hand, so I skip it.

The bell rings, trilling through the chatter, the stamp of feet on the stairs.

My first class is the history of ancient Greece. Mr. Noll writes the timeline of the Peloponnesian

War — 431–404 BC — on the blackboard. I wonder if Bozek is in the same mathematics class as Danika. I wonder if they're passing notes when Mrs. Hathazy's back is turned. If they're risking standing in the corner for passing notes.

A new and horrifying thought comes to me that maybe I won't find her after school. Maybe he'll whisk her away. And then I remember her violin lesson at Lada's house. Lada, the girl with the braces and thick ankles who plays first violin with the orchestra. Lada, who gives lessons in her apartment on a narrow side street.

"In the Peloponnesian War, democratic Athens was roundly defeated and dominated by oligarchic Sparta," says Mr. Noll.

Like us now with Russia, I think. I wonder if Mr. Noll is trying to let us know that he can't stand the stinking Russians. I look at him more closely with his curly blond sheep hair. Is he a *real* teacher and not just a propaganda machine?

But then Mr. Noll says the Spartans were strong and disciplined, and I understand that I got my hopes way too high. He likes the occupying Soviet Russians just fine.

At break time, when we march around the

gymnasium, Danika marches in the opposite direction, and as we pass, I catch her eye and make a funny face. She makes a funny face back. But she thinks we are just being kids together.

Bozek marches on the opposite side of the gymnasium, swinging his arms with gusto.

In my last class, which is botany, I tell the teacher I have a dentist appointment.

Mr. Ninzik asks, "Where is the note from your mother or father?"

I pretend to look in my pockets while hating doing this to Mr. Ninzik, who is the only teacher I like. He's the kind of guy who would hate the Spartans. I shrug, saying, "I can't find it." I open my mouth and point to a back molar: *"Cavity."*

He looks out the window and back at me and nods.

I grab my books and head out the door, down the hallway and stairs and outside, where I lie in wait beside a lilac bush, my heart thumping like a dog's leg when it scratches fleas.

The bell rings, and kids start to come out. I put my hand on my heart to keep the sound in. Will she come out with Bozek? Will he be telling her all about the wonders of Bratislava, where you can hear little snatches of Beatles songs and where boys have electric guitars and play the Beatles — muffled in a back room — whenever they want. With no Mrs. Zeman banging on the ceiling.

But no. Today is the day of the violin lesson. She must go to Lada's. It wouldn't be right to keep Lada waiting.

What Kind of Surprise?

She comes out, the sun full on her face, the violin case in her hand. My heart spins, swirls, stops, then marches on. There is no Bozek by her side.

I step out, hoping Mr. Ninzik isn't looking out the window.

"Patrik! What are you doing here?"

I take her violin case again, my sweat soaking the handle. "I'm here to walk you to Lada's."

"But you don't *have* to."

"I want to."

Out of the corner of my eye, I see Bozek coming down the steps, surrounded by boys who want to hear more about Bratislava and the Beatles.

"I have a surprise for you," I say, hurrying her away with the violin case banging against my leg. There's a tiny park on the way to Lada's.

"What kind of surprise?" she asks.

"You'll see." Out of habit I'm about to set down the violin case and books and yank my red scarf off. But then I don't. Danika is still wearing hers and seems to like it.

We come to the park blooming with tulips, and I say, "Let's go through here."

"But that will make me late, Patrik. Lada won't . . ."

"Let's go through here," I order. "I have something to tell you."

"If it's about Dr. Machovik, I already know."

"It's not about him. Not at all." I head for the fountain.

"I'm going to be *late*," she complains, but follows. She has to because I have the violin.

I sit down on the edge of the fountain. In the middle, a stone cherub is peeing, his pee splish-splashing from one level to another. "Come here."

She sits and smooths her skirt. But she's a little away from me, not like she would be with Bozek.

There's no time to waste. "I love you," I say.

She shrugs. "I love you, too."

"But not like that. Not how we used to love each other, Danika. Not like before . . ."

She looks at me then, looks in a way that I can tell she's forgotten about her violin lesson. She looks at my face and then her eyes move down, over the red scarf at my neck, over my chest, where my heart is trying to break loose. Her eyes settle on my hands, which are sweating buckets. I wipe them on my knees.

Her bright-blue eyes come back to my face. She wrinkles her forehead, then runs one hand over it. A breeze blows, knocking drops of cherub pee this way and that.

Suddenly she giggles. She puts a hand to her mouth. "Oh, my," she says through her hand.

My blood zooms like a million cars on a racetrack.

She takes her hand away from her mouth. She stops giggling. She reaches that hand — trembling — for my shoulder. "This *is* a surprise, Patrik. You've always been like a brother to me."

"Not anymore. I don't feel like a brother anymore," I protest. "I like you in a different way."

She drops her hand and looks at it lying limp in her lap.

"You're trying to tell me that you like Bozek instead of me? Is that it?" I drive the words hard.

"Don't be silly."

"What, then?" I kick at a weed sprouting between the paving stones.

"You and I used to play Gypsies together. Becoming your girlfriend would feel weird."

"It's because of Bozek."

"It's not. It's just that you've always been my friend. And you always will be."

Only that.

Pissing on Lenin

It's nighttime and I lean back against the square base of Lenin's statue. I imagine a nuclear missile coming straight from the U.S. of A.—even with me here—to blast Lenin. The missile would explode in a million red bits, bursting all over like the embers of a campfire. Then Lenin and I would be no more.

My thoughts revolve back to Danika. Obviously she likes Bozek instead of me. Bozek, the son of a party member. The son of a guy like Dr. Machovik, who sends his colleagues to hard labor. How *could* she?

Something goes *pop, pop* inside me.

I look around for Karel and Emil, who promised to meet me here. Where are they? Running a toy train? Listening one more time to the Beatles?

Karel especially should be coming. Adam Uherco is his distant relative. He should be here for Adam because Adam can't be.

At last, I make out Karel sidling along like a sideways-walking crab. "Where's Emil?" I ask. "I thought he was coming with you."

"Don't know. We said ten sharp right here. . . ."

"Maybe he's turned us in." I laugh, but both of us look around for searchlights, someone hunting us down. There's nothing. Nobody. Not even a moon.

"Emil wouldn't do that," Karel says.

"He probably just got cold feet," I say. "Let's do it without him. The longer we wait, the more chance there is of getting caught."

"I drank three glasses of water," Karel says.

"I gulped down a pot of tea."

We climb onto the base, right at Lenin's feet. Karel starts to unzip.

"Not down here," I say. "Up there." I point at the dark statue.

"Piss on his face?" Karel asks.

"Why not?" If America refuses to send that missile, my pee is the next best thing.

Karel links his fingers together, making a step with

his hands. He hoists me up the cold, slippery statue. I make my way onto the crooked-back elbow.

"Now, how do *I* get up?" Karel asks, his voice high.

"Like this." Securing my leg in Lenin's elbow, I reach down and grab Karel's hand. I yank him. He dangles, then gets a grip and hauls himself onto the statue's outstretched arm.

"I'm not giving up on Danika," I tell Karel.

From his perch, he says, "Don't torture yourself, Patrik. I've seen the way she looks at Bozek. . . ."

"But she knows me better. She's loved me all these years."

"She loves you like a friend."

"That can change. I can change it." And then I know I can't. I shove at Lenin's immovable shoulder with the toe of my green-spotted shoe. I shove harder, Karel watching from his own Lenin arm. When I start up a low growl, he says, "Come on."

So we unzip.

I feel the release, hear the splash of two streams of pee hitting metal. Both of us aim right onto the face. The pee runs into Lenin's eyes, down his metal beard. It drips onto his vest.

The *pop, pop* grows softer.

I zip up.

Karel pulls something from his pocket. "My sister's," he says, holding up a bra.

"That's not going to fit . . ."

"How about over the eyes?"

"Ha! That's good."

Working together, we pull the bra across Lenin's metal face, manage to hook it behind the head.

A car starts up nearby. We slither down. At the bottom, I pick up a stick and write in the dirt: REMEMBER ADAM UHERCO.

"Bravo," Karel says, then glances into the night as if looking for Adam. Or for those who locked him up.

"No one's out there," I whisper. "No one."

We slap each other's palms, then dash off into our own separate blackness.

By morning, the bra is gone. A garden hose lies coiled at the base of the statue, and puddles of clear water pool on the paving stones.

The Bra

Mr. Babicak's secretary summons me to the office. *This isn't fair,* I think, following her down the hallway. If only Danika had said yes, I wouldn't have done such a stupid thing. And why pick on me? I'm not the only one here who hates Lenin.

The white bra — very plain, no lace or frills — is lying on Babicak's desk. Beside it stands a jar filled with pencils and the sharp blade of a letter opener.

As soon as I'm seated, Mr. Babicak comes to the point. "You are playing into the hands of the imperialist Americans," he says. "Did you know that the Americans are aggressors throughout the world, Patrik? Did you know they are developing nuclear weapons?"

I nod. I won't point out that Russia is also building missiles and bombs. Not if I want to keep my head, I won't.

Mr. Babicak lifts the bra and dangles it from the tip of his pencil. "I think you know where this was found," he says, his beetly brows inching together.

This is a trick question. Everyone knows. It was Bozek, I hear, who climbed up to fetch the bra. Bozek Estochin who patriotically turned it in to the office. Everyone in school is giggling about this bra. If I say I don't know, Mr. Babicak will mock me. If I say I do, he'll pounce on me. So I say nothing.

"What about it, Chrobak?" His voice scoots across the desk.

"It's not mine, sir. I don't own a bra."

With a snort, he drops the bra back down. The hook clicks lightly on the wood. "Don't be a smart aleck, Chrobak."

A fine rain has been falling since early morning. Washing away fingerprints. No one saw us. Babicak can't prove anything. Without proof, I can't be locked up.

To my surprise, he says, "This will of course go on your record." He reaches for the jar, where I think he means to pick out a pencil. Instead his hand closes over the sharp letter opener. He runs his hand over the smooth blade.

I should keep my mouth shut. But I can't help myself. "But that's not right, sir," I say, putting both hands flat on his wide desk. "Nothing has been proven against me."

Babicak gives a bitter laugh. "I don't have to *prove* anything, young man. I only have to suspect. And"—he aims his glassy eyes upon me—"I strongly suspect." He lays down the letter opener, takes a piece of paper from the drawer and a pencil from the jar, and begins to write.

To have a permanent black mark on my record is even worse than copying *The Communist Manifesto*. I could be locked up after all.

The next day, Tati throws another paper down on the dining-room table. "This one I refuse to process," he says. "This is my colleague Dr. Albrecht. I absolutely refuse."

I stare at the paper. It's a little crumpled, as if Tati balled it up, then straightened it out. Is Mr. Babicak somehow responsible for this new order? Has he taken his revenge so swiftly? "What will happen to Dr. Albrecht?" I ask.

"He's to be put away in a mental institution. No better than prison."

"No tractor driving?"

Tati shakes his head. "He might still open his mouth and say things the party doesn't want said."

"Maybe he'll see Adam Uherco at that place," I say.

Tati presses his lips together.

Mami glances at the window.

Last week a man washed those windows, using a rag on a long pole. It could have been Dr. Csider doing the washing. Except he is way up by Prikra.

Maybe someone has planted a bug. And now somewhere a man is huddled in an office, listening to our conversation. Recording it for proof with a reel-to-reel tape recorder.

Mami yanks back the curtain. Maybe the window washer was really a high-up party spy. Maybe he planted a microphone. She runs her fingertip along the frame, perhaps checking for wires. She tries to open the window, but it's corroded shut.

"What will happen to you, Tati?" I ask, moving closer. "To us?"

"I hardly care anymore," Tati says.

"You have to care about the children," says Mami

gently. She turns on the radio, perhaps to cover up our conversation.

The broadcaster announces that the Soviet spacecraft Luna 10 is still orbiting the moon. This makes the Soviet Russians very proud. But what is *really* going on — friends turning against one another, people being certified as crazy, school principals terrorizing their students, students fighting back in little, stupid ways — of that the Soviet Russians will tell us nothing.

Just as the Russians hold back secrets, so do I. Babicak has no proof against me. There's nothing for me to confess to Tati. And yet I now have that black mark. I should tell Tati to watch his back. I really should.

The Forest

In botany, Mr. Ninzik stands with his jacket on, gripping the massive tome of *Trees of the Western Slovakian Forests*. "We're going on a field trip today, boys and girls."

Murmurs. No one ever takes us out of here.

"I'll be accompanying you and my third-period class to the Bazima Forest. We're going to identify trees. Please bring notebooks and pencils."

I do a quick calculation of Danika's schedule, and yes, she and I will be in the forest together. Bozek will probably be back at school studying the Peloponnesian War.

We gather in the hallway in lines, each of us in an assigned spot. When the other kids join us, I wave at

Danika and smile. She smiles back — beaming widely. She's smiling. No turning away from me.

Maybe, just maybe, she's already changed her mind. An unforeseen miracle has come to pass. The whole world suddenly feels just right.

We walk single file down the street, Danika and I separated from each other by eleven students. I count and count again those who separate us. The overhead flutter of the red flags, the yellow-hammer-and-sickle Communist flags, almost makes me happy.

Entering the forest, Mr. Ninzik waves, signaling that we're liberated. He sets down the heavy field guide and strolls off with his hands in his pockets. He obviously doesn't really care if we identify a darn thing. He's brought us here to get away from school and all the propaganda. We dump our notebooks into a giant pile.

I make my way to Danika. But I don't stand too close. Not yet. "Remember how we used to play cowboys and Indians here?" I gesture toward the trees, the spotty shadows along the forest floor, the bushes in bloom.

She smiles like old times, as if we'd never had the talk beside the fountain. "My favorite was playing Partisans against Nazi Germans."

"How about Janosik?"

"All of you guys fought over who would get to be him," she says. "Over who had to be just one of his men."

"Or worse, who had to be the one getting robbed. Remember how you were all three witches at once?"

She laughs, then lowers her pretty face to gaze at the pine needles. As the witches, Danika bestowed upon us the magical staff—a tree branch—and the magical shirt and belt, both borrowed from her father's closet. She handed these things to whoever was playing Janosik, announcing with big drama, "Now you have the power to escape all traps."

I head toward the stream, praying that she'll follow me. She hesitates only a moment, looking into the treetops.

We take the path that parallels the stream, where the water glides over the yellow shallows. The woods fill with shouts and the smoke of newly lit cigarettes. When we arrive at the place where the stream tumbles thickly, darkly over the boulders, I stop. Still keeping my distance, I look down onto her light hair, saying, "It wouldn't be weird, Danika."

She wrinkles her forehead, as if confused. Then she shakes her head ever so slightly. Even before she speaks, the chill of the forest closes in. "It would," she says firmly. "It would be very weird."

"Other kids used to be just friends and now they're boyfriend and girlfriend. Just look at Erik and Libena."

She sits down on a square, mossy rock. "It's something other than that, Patrik. There's something bigger happening."

"What, then?" What could possibly be bigger? I lean against the trunk of a pine. The irregular, puzzle-piece bark imprints itself on my back.

She takes a deep breath, then says, "A few days ago, my father was invited to join the party."

This knocks the wind out of me. "And?" Surely, Mr. Holub has said no. He's always seemed like a decent, levelheaded guy.

"He's joining."

"That's terrible news." I look around at the tumbling stream, at the silly clumps of lilacs. "Joining the party means spying on others. Like your neighbors. Like your friends and family. If someone doesn't spy, he goes to prison."

"I know all that."

"You know it, and yet . . . ?" Between the trees, the blue sky glares at us.

"Sometimes things like that are necessary," Danika says in a small voice.

"Dr. Machovik has already sent a colleague of his, a friend of his, off to do roadwork."

"He probably had good reason," she says primly.

I stare at her, my childhood friend gone wrong.

She rubs her hands together, as if trying to warm them. "My mother says we've been poor too long. By joining the party, Tati will get a higher-paying job."

"A fine motive."

"Stop it, Patrik. You don't know how we eat day-old bread. And we hardly ever get butter or meat."

"What about people like Adam Uherco? What about him?"

"Sometimes . . ."

I kneel down beside her, my face close to hers. "So you'd betray people to eat better? Is that it?"

"Don't say that."

"I'm right, though. Aren't I?"

She's silent, her lower lip shoved out. She picks up a leaf and twirls it by the stem.

"I get it. You're now forbidden to associate with someone like me. Someone who doesn't buy the party line."

"I can *associate* with you. I can be your friend."

Danika starts to tear the leaf along the veins, carefully, as if dissecting it for botany class. "But anything closer . . ."

I snatch the leaf from her hand. "And what do *you* think about this party that would keep you from me? What do *you* feel?"

"I don't know. Honestly, I don't." She picks up another leaf.

A new thought falls like a tree across my path. "You'd never betray me, would you? You'd never betray my family?"

She looks at me with her clear blue eyes. "Of course not, Patrik. Of course not."

"But you don't really know. Not yet, anyway." Her red scarf flares against the green forest. It's like a bullfighter's cape. It makes me feel like a mad bull.

At the shrill sound of Mr. Ninzik's whistle crisscrossing the forest, Danika rises from her rock. Perhaps she's relieved to be called back.

I block her way. "Is this why you were upset at Emil's a while back?"

She brushes the back of her skirt. "Maybe. Well, yes. You were all saying such mean things about the party. And I was confused. . . . But I'm not anymore. I've accepted Tati's decision."

She already sounds like a good Communist. "Danika . . ."

But she's gone past me, calling over her shoulder, "It's no use, Patrik."

I call after her, "Wearing that red scarf, you'll never be allowed into America. The Statue of Liberty doesn't hold out her flame for Communists."

Danika doesn't turn around.

On the way up the path, I take pictures of everything, pressing the shutter over and over. I capture a bird's fallen nest, tree trunks, lichen-covered rocks, the back of Danika's retreating head. I use up almost a whole roll of film, but I can't stop shooting.

On the march back to school, I leap up, almost ripping the red flags down.

All the Way Gone

A few days later, we come into botany to find Mr. Ninzik gone. Whiskery Mrs. Jakim, who taught us in grade school, stands in his place. She's peering into the textbook, running her finger under the lines.

"Someone turned Mr. Ninzik in," the boy behind me whispers. "He's not here anymore."

I look around, as if I might see Mr. Ninzik after all. The long fingers of the state have reached into our school. Who was the rat? Maybe Bozek, who so loves to wear his red scarf.

Or was it Danika?

The clomp of shoes again and Mr. Babicak enters. He picks up Mr. Ninzik's pointer. He taps it on the desk. Then he waves it, saying, "Mr. Ninzik has always been a secret enemy. All along Mr. Ninzik has bucked the revolution. Instead of taking you to the Bazima Forest to identify trees, to advance your scientific knowledge, to make you strong and disciplined citizens of the state, he let you play around."

Taking kids to the forest can't be it. Not the whole picture. Mr. Ninzik is gone because he's done something more than meets the eye. He hates the Spartans and would piss on Lenin if the night was dark enough.

Again, I glance toward the doorway, toward the windows.

"And now, thankfully, Mr. Ninzik has left," Mr. Babicak goes on, "and kind Mrs. Jakim is here to pull you back from the reactionary precipice." He taps the pointer again.

Kind Mrs. Jakim, my eyeball. When I was ten years old, the school had a campaign for Cuba, where Castro had pulled off a revolution. To stop America from attacking the new Communist nation, each of us had to put our allowance into the glass jar at the front of each classroom. Everyone could see how much you put in. How good a Communist you were. Mrs. Jakim watched extra hard to make sure we didn't try to fool her with a bottle cap instead of a coin.

I always dropped in just a few crowns, barely enough to look like a good Communist.

Mr. Babicak lets loose of the pointer and strides over to Libena Kaspar's desk. He gestures for her to lift her elbows off her black notebook.

She does so, her eyes big with surprise.

Mr. Babicak flips open the notebook. Grunting with satisfaction, he holds it up for all to see. Inside, Libena has glued clippings of pretty, dark-haired Sophia Loren and blond Brigitte Bardot with the big boobies.

"Look, boys and girls," he says with triumph. "Just look at these decadent Western film stars."

Some of us look. Even Mrs. Jakim tears her gaze from her frantic study of the botany textbook. Others stare off, looking anywhere but where Babicak orders them to look.

Mr. Babicak tucks the notebook under one arm, probably to put in Libena's record. By now Libena is wiping at tears with the ends of her Young Pioneer scarf.

Next, Mr. Babicak goes to Dalek's satchel. When he jerks it, tipping out the contents, American postal stamps scatter across the floor. The little faces of the

American presidents stare up at us. "Hah!" says Mr. Babicak, grinding the stamps underfoot. "Here you live in the greatest social experiment in the history of the world, and you hoard — shamelessly hoard — these worthless symbols of imperialism!"

"Gone just like that," Tati says about Mr. Ninzik, snapping his fingers. "You step over the line just the tiniest bit, and . . ." He snaps again.

Poor Mr. Ninzik is probably hauling wheelbarrows of gravel. Or he's just plain gone.

Sitting at the kitchen table, my geometry book spread open on the burgundy cloth, I concentrate harder on the proofs. It's logical, one-answer work.

"All the way gone," whispers Mami, meaning the freezing tundra of Siberia. In Siberia, where it's ice and snow and hard labor all year round.

I should tell my parents that Mr. Holub is joining the party. That soon he'll be a danger to all of us. But if I tell them, they'll never let Danika come to this apartment again.

The area of this triangle equals the area of that one. Even though they look so different.

"We have to get out of here," says Mami.

I keep my eyes pinned on my book.

The lines on Mami's forehead deepen. "Maybe you should go lecture in another country and not come back."

Mami always suggests this.

"But that would leave the rest of you stuck here in Trencin."

Tati always counters with this.

I blacken the triangle, then the polyhedron, my pencil scritch-scratching. I draw a tree from the Bazima Forest. I draw a cylinder around the tree, trapping it.

"It's hard to know what to do." Tati rubs his chin. He doesn't want to pump gas in Pennsylvania. He doesn't want to give up on being a psychiatrist.

But if Tati doesn't pump gas in America, he may end up doing something just as lowly here. He may collect garbage or drive a truck filled with bags of cement. In Pennsylvania he'd be pumping the gas for his own sake, not the state's.

I look at the walls, papered with a vague, off-white pattern. There could be hidden microphones in those walls. Sometimes the bugs are concealed under carpets, in furniture.

"Every day at the clinic," Mami says, also looking around, "people come in complaining of headaches and stomachaches. But really, they're just high-strung."

"They're all nervous," Tati says. "They're being watched."

I shut my geometry book, the half-finished proofs inside. Leaving Mami and Tati wandering in the maze of their escape plans, I retreat to the refuge of my dark-room. I develop the negative of LONG LIVE THE US ! I blow it up big.

A knock comes on the darkroom door. Without thinking, I call out, "It's okay. You can let in the light now."

The door opens, and there stands Danika. Over the years, she's often visited me here. I've even taught her a bit about developing. But I'm surprised to see her now. Has she — my heart cartwheels — come to see me? Not just see me, but *see* me?

Her face reflects in the red surface of the developing fluids. She looks past me to the photograph hanging by the clothespins. She studies the slogan with its two missing letters. Her eyes widen in the red light.

"You probably hope no one finds out about that," I say.

"Oh, you mean . . . Well, yes. I wish you'd tear that photo up."

"You're not in it. And I've already been punished." Her flowery scent fills the darkroom, mixing with the acid smell of the chemicals.

She sighs, then studies the other negatives — pictures of the Bazima Forest, the back of her own head. Her eyes flit here and there.

"Do you still want this?" I hold up one of the prints I made of the Beatles' faces.

"Sure," she says, but takes the print slowly, without enthusiasm.

Suddenly, I realize what she's really come for. The precious thing she's risked seeing me to get. My jaw tightens. I take her image from where it's pinned on the back of the door, the image with Bozek's face cut away.

She reaches for it, then draws her hand back.

"You're wondering where Bozek is."

"Well, yes . . ."

"I cut his face off."

"You're joking."

I shrug. "I'm the photographer."

Danika picks up a loose clothespin and snaps it open. Snaps it shut. "I didn't know you were so petty, Patrik."

"It was an artistic decision." I kick at the waste-basket. "He's in there somewhere. You're welcome to look."

She pinches her finger with the clothespin, then throws it down.

Thistles

With Karel off at his model-train club, Emil and I decide to ride the bus to the castle perched on the hill above town. When you want to escape everything, a castle is a good place.

At the last bus stop, Emil and I get out at the ancient ruins. Castles are everywhere, left over from the times of the Roman Empire, and on this one the inscription reads: *We Romans were here in the name of Pax Romana 200 AD.* But now no one is supposed to be here because the walls could collapse. Following Emil, I wander in on a path overgrown with thistles. The prickly leaves graze my hands, lightly scratching them.

I walk over the broken glass of smashed liquor bottles, over crushed beer cans. "Careful," says Emil, peering through the massive entry. "There could be police."

Instead of looking into the castle, I glance behind. A man pulls up in a dirty white Volkswagen Beetle. The car has a large patch of rust on the fender.

There aren't any police inside, but I still go cautiously, half expecting to find Danika and Bozek kissing here. Mushing up against each other. Under the spreading tree, with its dark-purple shade, would be a perfect spot.

But only a few boys are playing a game in the open courtyard. Heat waves rise off the paving stones. The game is part soccer, part handball, as the boys kick the ball against the castle wall. The ball wallops the wall of slogans: *Down with all Fascist dogs!* and *Invaders out!*

The walls are also covered with love hearts. I scan the ruined surfaces for two sets of initials. But they're not here. Which means nothing.

"Want to join in?" Emil asks, nodding toward the game.

Part of me wants to. It would feel good to hurl and slam a ball. But part of me feels as fragile as the castle itself. "Go ahead."

Emil shakes his head.

The driver of the VW strolls into the castle courtyard. He wears a beige Windbreaker and has beige hair to match.

I lead the way to the edge of the precipice. The pale buildings and red roofs of Trencin lie tiny before us. From here the city looks peaceful, not at all like a nest of traitors and spies. There's the river, my school, even our gray apartment building along with all the others.

Somewhere down there lives the tiny figure of Danika, smaller than Bela's doll.

"It looks like a bunch of toys," says Emil.

"Or like a dream. As a kid, I had flying dreams. I used to fly like this." I hold my arms straight out. With my eyes closed, I imagine myself soaring over Trencin.

Emil pulls out a cigarette and lights it. Then, blowing smoke rings, he says slowly, "I think a lot of people want to fly. Fly away, I mean."

Emil's words, along with the smoke, come to me as though in a dream. I open my eyes and cast him a glance. Is he saying that *he* wants to fly away? Are his steel-mill parents making plans? Maybe all of us are poised for flight.

There's now a hitch in our own plan. Tati got a letter from his aunt. With the big new highway, not enough cars stop at their gas station. Our Slovakian family in America will have to close the station down.

So there will be no jobs pumping gas for us.

The man in beige moves closer. He adjusts his lapel, maybe turning on a tiny tape recorder.

"How about you?" Emil asks, dislodging a rock with his shoe.

"I'm fine. Except for Danika."

"Hmm," Emil muses, blowing three perfect gray halos. He pushes the rock, and it clatters all the way down.

He wants to talk more. I can tell. I also want to talk. I want to tell him how Danika's father is joining the party. But then Emil wouldn't like her anymore. I want to tell him that my parents are feeling their way through a labyrinth, looking for a way out, bumping against dead ends.

But even Emil could change in the blink of an eye. I think of Dr. Machovik. Even Emil could turn against me.

Flames

Bela and Mami sit at the kitchen table, a pile of paper flowers stacked in front of them. Bela wears one of the flowers behind her ear. All morning they've been cutting and twisting the paper, preparing the decorations. On the day before May Day, a person like Bozek will walk the streets with a clipboard, marking down which windows are bare.

Someone knocks on our front door, and I open up to see Bozek, a pile of flags draped over one arm, a bag slung over the other. Bozek of all people. He puts a foot in the doorway, as if I might close him out.

"Is your family ready?" he asks.

"We're working on it." I move closer, using my beanpole height against him. I reach down for a flag of each country, thinking that later Mami can clean the furniture with the Russian one.

"Make sure you hang the Russian flag," Bozek says. "It doesn't matter so much about the Czechoslovakian, but do hang the Russian flag."

"I know." He thinks I'm a moron.

Bozek lifts the paper bag, and I hear the clank of metal. "Do you have flag holders?"

"Of course we do. From last year and the year before and before . . ." He thinks we're all morons.

He lingers. He's no doubt looking for something suspicious. Like my photo of the painted-out letters. Maybe he suspects that Danika is here.

"Do you have something else to give us?" I ask.

He shrugs.

Thwack, I close the door on him. I open it again and look out. But he's already at old Mr. and Mrs. Smutny's door.

"I hate to think of who made these," says Mami, stretching out the flags.

"Who?" Bela wants to know.

"Prisoners," Mami answers. "And not even criminals. Ordinary people. Anyone who says boo to the state."

"That's sad," Bela says, taking the flower out of her hair and adding it to the others.

"It is indeed," Mami agrees. "Help me, Patrik. Let's get these flags hung."

"Be sure to go today, Patrik. Don't hide out. And sing. Don't just mouth the words," Tati advises me. "It's hard to stomach, I know . . . but for the sake of all of us . . ." He straightens my red scarf, making sure it lies neatly. "There will be a lot of secret agents milling about," he says. "Ready to pounce on anyone who doesn't look enthused."

"I promise to look enthused," I assure him. Babicak will certainly have his eye on me.

Out in the street, the crowd has already gathered. Lining up are the steelworkers, with Danika's father and Emil's parents among them, the workers from the local spa, those who bottle the spa's water, the professors from the university, the Communist militia, Tati and the other psychiatrists of Western Slovakia, and the doctors from the hospital. But not Dr. Csider, who told one too many jokes.

Tractors decked out with red flags have arrived from the collective farms. If I knew Eduard Bagin by sight, I'd look for him. Party members carry more red flags, raising the poles high. Women in Slovakian dancing costumes look ready to lift their embroidered skirts, kick up their legs, and prance.

High above the crowd float big photo portraits of famous Communists: Lenin, Karl Marx, Fidel Castro, and Lumumba of the Congo. The giant faces stare down on us, watching. Watching for those who might pee on them.

Secret agents are certainly mixed into the crowd. Rumor has it that for every two people, there's one agent. We never know who. As Mami likes to say, it could be the butcher, the baker, the candlestick maker.

Three police vans, their windows blacked out, are parked at the corner.

At school, Mami leads Bela by the hand, helping her find a spot at the front of the parade. The younger kids are dressed in their white shirts, the older in blue. Of course, all of us sport the pointy red scarves. Mami blows a kiss to Bela, then hurries off to find the other nurses.

Mr. Babicak, Mr. Noll, Mrs. Jakim, and the other teachers stand with clipboards and pens. The principal calls out names, and we take our places in formation. I'm next to Bozek. He stands serious, his haircut shorter than before. For this special day, he's wearing a pair of blue jeans. I move toward the boy on my left.

Through a gap in the buildings, I see a caravan of Gypsy wagons winding along a distant hillside. They don't have to march in this stupid parade but are making their own. Even the Communist Party has no hold over them. *Outside of proper society,* people say.

A shifty, restless feeling grows among us. Some of us are eager to begin the celebration; others want to get it done with. It's hard to know who feels what.

Four boys and four girls carry the banners that stretch the width of the street. When Mr. Babicak finally blows the whistle, they unfurl and we set off.

The parade has begun. We're a few steps closer to the end.

As the parade moves out of range of the teachers' control, some of us break formation, edging nearer to friends. I sidle close to Emil and Karel. Together we march behind a flag with dangling red fringe.

On each street corner, bands play the Communist anthem, "The Internationale." "Arise, ye workers from your slumber . . ." Loudspeakers blare: "Soviet Union forever!" We wave—we have to wave—at those lining the streets, mostly the mothers. Although they have no official group to march with, they have to be here.

Since I also have to be here, I wish I was at least marching with Danika. If she was my girlfriend, I could put up with this. Just as I think that, I catch sight of her. She's not far ahead.

She's walking with Bozek. Two good Commies marching together. So it's come to this. I bite the inside of my cheek on one side, then the other.

"Don't look," says Karel. "Don't get yourself upset."

He's right. I shouldn't look. Not with that black mark on my record.

Emil presses something small into my hand. I open my fingers to his plastic cigarette lighter.

Walking on tiptoe, I see that those two are not only marching together. They're holding hands.

Karel points at the red fringe on the flag ahead of us.

I glance toward the giant faces of famous Communists. All but one — Lumumba — are facing away. I flick the tiny wheel of the lighter. It takes a few seconds for the fringe to catch. I hold the lighter steady, my thumb firm. Finally, the fire ripples along.

Karel and Emil dash off, but I stick around. I raise my camera to the flag on fire and shoot, capturing the glorious moment.

The man holding the flag touches the back of his

neck. He whips the flag around and drops it to the ground. He stamps out the flames.

A bunch of people stare, one shouts, and then the parade goes on, the man carrying the blackened flag in his arms.

I move away, looking around for anyone who might know me. That man over there—is he the one from the castle, the one with the beige jacket and the VW Beetle? Now he's wearing a dark-blue jacket, so it's hard to be sure.

The parade makes a turn onto a side street where no one's watching. The marching bands play a few more bars of melody and fall silent. Thank God the marching peters out.

I run across Mr. Ninzik, who is not with any group. He hasn't been sent to the wastelands of Siberia after all. He's not shoveling rocks and ice. At least not yet. "Mr. Ninzik!" I call.

He looks around, hands shoved deep into his pockets.

"Mr. Ninzik!" I wave. I want to tell him that I've just acted against the state. I've rebelled. In the name of Adam Uherco and of all of us. "Mr. Ninzik!"

He smiles briefly. When I get right up to him, he says, his mouth barely moving, "Don't be seen with me, Patrik. It won't be good for you."

So I look at the ground, then past him. I pretend I've never met him before. Lighting the flag on fire was stupid. It didn't do anyone any good. It was all for myself. Striking a match wasn't like whatever Mr. Ninzik probably did to get himself kicked out of the school.

I walk away. When I look again, Mr. Ninzik is gone.

I turn to see Danika walking alongside a float with flowers arranged to form a gigantic hammer and sickle. Bozek marches beside her.

The float stops, and Bozek begins to lift the little kids down. Danika takes each one by the hand and finds the right mother. Bozek lifts. Danika delivers. The two make a good team.

I grab a hunk of flowers off a float that's stopped near me. I grab another hunk. I make a big hole in the hammer and sickle. I mash the petals, then throw the handfuls down. I'm tearing at more flowers when a mother asks, "What are you *doing,* young man?"

"Nothing," I answer, grinding the flowers under my shoe. "I'm doing nothing."

Birds on a Hill

Bela wants white icing for the cookies, but Mami tells her there's no extra sugar.

"Even if you stood in line for it?" Bela asks.

"Not even if I stood for hours and hours."

Karel, Emil, and I are sitting on the couch, watching a Charlie Chaplin movie for the hundredth time.

"How can that guy be a party member?" Karel asks. He's been tinkering with a tiny train engine, trying to straighten the wheels.

"He's too goofy for it," Emil says.

"And yet . . ."

Karel and Emil have had this discussion about a hundred times before.

Bela comes in, licking batter off a big spoon. While Charlie Chaplin studies himself in the many mirrors, she runs around bowlegged, holding a pretend hat, copying him.

"Bela, get out of here." I swipe at her imaginary hat.

"It's my house, too."

"Go away."

She sticks her tongue out.

I smell the cookies baking, a sweet stickiness spreading through the apartment.

When Bela leaves, I whisper, "Danika has a big secret."

"What's that?" Karel asks, leaning forward, the small engine in one hand.

I look to the windows for peering faces. I listen to make sure that Bela is safely back in the kitchen, chattering to Mami. I beckon my friends even closer. "Her father's joining the party."

Emil whistles.

Karel sucks in air, then says, "Now Mr. Holub will be watching us."

"Danika will rat us out," Emil says.

I wish I could assure them she never would.

Karel asks, "Do your parents know?"

I hold a finger to my lips. "They mustn't find out. If they knew, they'd never let Danika come here."

Karel makes a show of looking around. "I don't see her here now."

I punch him on the shoulder, but lightly.

"Who wants her here, anyway?" Karel asks. "She's tight with that Commie."

I punch Karel harder this time.

"Let's get out of here," says Emil. "Let's go to my house. Listen to the Beatles."

Karel makes a face. "And get tortured by your neighbor? How about downtown instead?" He pauses, looking from Emil to me. *"We can chat up some stray pie,"* he adds in English. Having learned this phrase from Emil's older cousin, he uses it often.

I hesitate. Ever since the flag burning, I've been nervous about going out. What if people from the parade recognize me? What if they call the police? *This boy committed a dastardly deed. . . .*

But my two friends are already headed for the door. Not wanting to be left behind like the little red engine Karel set down on the table, I follow.

Mami calls out, "Cookies will be ready in a minute."

I pause. A warm cookie would be nice. But Emil and Karel are already pounding down the stairs. "Later," I answer. "Later they'll taste great."

Two men I've never seen are standing near the building. One is talking into a walkie-talkie.

The bus is leaving the corner, so we run down the

walkway and along the street. Emil knocks hard on the closed doors, and, with a sour expression, the driver opens up. We climb aboard and plunk a few coins into the slot. Then we stamp our way to the back seats, where the smokers hang out, where kids make out, and where the seats are higher.

As the bus pulls forward, I look through the back window to see that the two men are both focusing on the bus. For a second, I lock eyes with one of them. He knows. Surely he knows about me.

The bus rolls through town, picking up passengers, letting them off. I snap photos of people, pigeons, streetcars, hiding my face behind the bulky black camera.

At the center of town, where the streets narrow, where the mushroom-colored buildings poke their red roofs into the sky, we get off. As the accordion doors open and I descend the metal steps, I look around. Who on this crowded street might be an enemy? But no one looks my way. I follow Emil and Karel passing a collective, where women hunch over sewing machines, and a state-run store selling radios and chocolates.

A crowd has gathered. We move closer until Karel mutters, "Thunderbird." Emil and Karel climb the base of a lamppost while I stay down, peeking through people at the ice-blue car with the tiny, round porthole.

Low to the ground, sleek as a wet otter, it must go really fast. This is what people drive in America.

"Come," Karel calls to me. "The view is great."

I glance around again. No one's paying attention to me. I climb up to stare down at the gleaming roof of the blue Thunderbird.

Suddenly I see Bozek and Danika in the crowd below. Danika and Bozek. Weaving in and out, headed for the Thunderbird. They're not just holding hands. They have each other by the waists.

"Hell," I mutter, knotting up my fists.

"Let's go this way," Karel says. Pulling on my arm, he yanks me off my perch. He leads me toward a side street.

"Don't." I free my arm. "I can take it."

"In here," says Emil, pushing me into a doorway. It's a tavern filled with the sounds of Beach Boys music—a song about girls in the faraway state of California. Soldiers in stiff brown uniforms are dancing with young women. A mirrored ball twirls on the ceiling, casting sparkly lights along the floor, the bar stools, the faces of the dancers.

I want to get back out to the street, take another look, but my friends block the way. From here I can see the bartender polishing a glass with a white towel. It's not his job to kick out thirteen-year-olds.

"There's lots of girls in here," says Karel. "Take your pick. Forget Danika."

He's right. There are a couple of pretty girls. One is even wearing a miniskirt.

We move into the crowd. We stay far from the eyes of the bartender, who's chatting up the woman in the miniskirt. Now the Beach Boys are singing about surfing. The floor vibrates with the beat. If I ever get to the U.S.A., I'll surf in Scranton, Pennsylvania. I picture Danika dressed in a bikini. I picture us surfing together.

Hell, hell, hell . . .

Emil moves over to a girl with long carmel-colored hair and asks her something. She nods and they move onto the dance floor.

"Your turn," says Karel.

I shake my head. No way.

"Come on. You're so tall. You look even older than we do."

The miniskirt girl has moved away from the bartender. She's coming across the floor, her face not as pretty as her legs.

Karel shoves me forward.

When the girl gets close, I think of Danika with her arm around Bozek's waist and utter just one word: "Dance?"

She looks up into my face, her eyelashes laden with black makeup. Her lipstick shines pinky white. Then she says, her words a little slurred, "Sure, kid. Why not?"

Karel stands by the wall, grinning. Emil twists with his long-haired partner.

At that moment, the music changes from fast Beach Boys to a slow Beatles song we hardly ever hear. Paul McCartney sings about birds on a hill. I hadn't bargained on a slow song. The girl, woman really, steps toward me. I hold up one hand to take hers, ballroom-style.

But instead of taking the hand I offer, she slips both arms around my shoulders. Though her head comes just to my chin, I'm taken into her world of silky warmth, perfume, and beer fumes. The black light comes on, making everyone's eyeballs glow.

I try not to think of Danika. I try not to think of her dancing like this with Bozek. I try not to think of her whispering secrets in his ear.

I step on my partner's foot.

"Ouch!" she exclaims, drawing back slightly. "What's wrong with you?"

I release my grip on her waist. "I'm sorry. This isn't a good time. . . ."

She shoves me away, her teeth glinting. "Make up your mind, kid. Next time, don't ask until you're sure."

On the way home, I go into the Foto-Kino shop to buy a roll of film. Inside, the shelves are full of bottles of chemicals for developing. Two cameras sit displayed in a glass case.

When I ask for film, the young woman shakes her head. "There's no film. None at all." She pinches her eyebrows together.

"Not even one roll?"

"There's no film in the whole city."

I slap the counter. Stupid government. Always a shortage of something. Then I lower my voice. "Not even on the black market?"

"Not even."

I must have film. How else will I get through the days? Slowly, I count out my allowance on the counter, enough for ten rolls at normal prices.

At first, the woman looks puzzled. Then her pale

fingers close around the bills, bundling them into her fist. With her head tilted down, she looks up at me, her mascara a little smeared.

I meet those eyes without blinking. I need film.

Without a word, the woman goes to the back room. I hear her dial the telephone. Hear her speak muffled words. She comes back out, saying, "Go to the corner. Someone will come."

"How will they know me?"

"I told them you're tall."

Out on the corner, I tap the light pole. *Tappa-tap-tap.* Standing here in the open, I feel naked. So many people driving and walking by. Any of them could say, *Aha! There's that boy. That flag burner.*

My hands itch for the feel of the small orange box. Or maybe the film won't be inside a box. Maybe just a black canister. Black and perfectly smooth, with a coil of treasure inside.

Tappa-tap-tap.

I've stepped out of line, like Adam Uherco. I've made myself a target. And here I am exposed and alone, with no friends standing nearby.

But I can't think about that. Instead I imagine opening my camera, unwinding the end of the film, tucking it in, snapping the camera tight. With film I could record the world, feeling that special power in my hands.

A group of young girls passes, giggling. Businessmen with briefcases. A soldier from the disco. A Gypsy stands out in her long, flowered skirt, hoop earrings, and bright kerchief. If only I had my camera. I'd capture this woman, show her to Danika later on. . . .

People come near, but no one swerves close. No one comes to me grasping a precious roll of film.

Tappa-tap-tap.

I walk back to the shop. A CLOSED sign hangs in the window. I peer in, but there's no trace of the saleswoman.

At the corner by my building, two new men stand guard. I see the bulges of walkie-talkies in their jacket pockets. They know. They know all about me.

Room 129

"A letter arrived for you, Patrik," says Mami when I come in from school. She holds out a slim white envelope.

I never get mail. I drop my book satchel onto the floor and take the letter. Sure enough, here's my name in black-and-white across the front: *Patrik Chrobak*. The return address is that of the Trencin police station. "Did you open this?" I ask Mami, examining the seal, which has obviously been broken and glued back together. She needs Mr. Babicak's sharp letter opener.

"I did, Patrik. I'm so sorry. But I couldn't stand the suspense. It's an order to appear."

I rip open the envelope. The letter contains just one line. As Mami said, I'm to go at ten o'clock the next morning to room 129 of the downtown police station. It doesn't say what about.

That evening, while Mami is putting Bela to bed, I wash my plate, then my silverware and drinking glass. I take my time, sudsing up, rinsing, even drying. At last, with nothing possible left to do, I go to the living room.

Tati is reading the newspaper. Beside my ripped-open summons, his pipe lies idle in the ashtray, with his little pouch of tobacco nearby.

Putting my hands on my hips, I get the announcement over with: "I know why I've been called in."

Tati looks up from the newspaper.

"During the May Day parade, I set fire to a flag." And there, I've said it. The words fall like tiny grenades into the lemony light.

Tati blinks, then says, "You can't be serious, Patrik. Please tell me this is a joke."

"It's not."

His face grows as red as the Communist flag. "I thought . . . I thought I cautioned you about that damn parade."

"You did. I couldn't help myself."

"Couldn't help yourself! What is that supposed to

mean?" Tati stands up, the newspaper falling to the floor, the pages skittering loose.

"I was upset."

He kicks the newspaper into a pile. "What kind of upset would make you do such an idiotic thing?"

"A girl."

"A girl? You'd do something like that over a *girl*?" He paces to the window, then back, saying, "This comes at a terrible time for me. I'm being pressured on all sides. And now this . . . this terrible news."

A silence falls between us. I melt into my shame. In the other room, Mami is singing lullabies to Bela.

When Mami's lullaby comes to an end, Tati says, "You'll wish you hadn't done that. Now there will be hell to pay. Pure hell."

With the back of my hand, I wipe my forehead.

Tati sits back down. He lights his pipe and turns the radio to the Voice of America. The language of the evening is perhaps Russian. But that's okay. What matters is that these broadcasters are on our side and against the Trencin police.

The broadcast ends, and music begins to play. I always hope for rock 'n' roll — the Beatles, or maybe the Rolling Stones — but it's jazz.

I sit down in the chair across from Tati's. The

broadcast turns back to talk, this time in Slovakian. Tati twists the dial a teeny bit, making the words louder. But as usual, a loud *wowoowowoo* sound blocks the broadcaster's voice.

I lean close but can't make out a thing.

Suddenly I say, "Don't talk in front of Danika. Don't say political things in front of her."

Tati raises his eyebrows.

"She wears her red scarf when she doesn't have to. She even wears it on weekends."

"I've never noticed her doing that," Tati says.

"It's only lately."

"We hardly see Danika anymore," Tati goes on. "Is she busy with school?"

"Very," I answer. I want to tell him about Mr. Holub. I really do.

In the morning, with the usual sour-faced driver at the wheel, Tati and I ride the bus downtown. We sit right up front, stiff in our good suits. As if nice clothes will do the trick. My hands sweat all over the letter.

Dirty washcloths of rain clouds heap together.

The police station is located in a big squarish building with flags flying. Eyeing the police vans packed together, I follow Tati. We mount the slick marble steps.

Inside, the building isn't so stately. Our footsteps echo under high ceilings with peeling, flag-size strips of paint. I wipe my hand along walls grubby with the handprints of others who've wiped along them. As we pass a janitor pushing a wide broom, I wonder if the man has always been a janitor, or whether he used to be a doctor or lawyer who spoke his mind. I hope Tati doesn't become a janitor.

Or—the thought suddenly strikes me like a bolt of lightning—I hope *I* don't become a janitor.

Then, in the distance of the long hallway, I see Dr. Machovik. The back of his curly head, the barely visible goatee. His slightly uneven gait. He turns down another hallway and is gone.

"Wasn't that Dr. Machovik?" I ask Tati.

"I didn't notice."

"Does he work in this building?"

"I believe he does."

We arrive at room 129, the number glaring blackly from the frosted-glass door. Tati turns the knob, and I push the door open. Secretaries sit at desks behind the counter, their typewriters click-clattering away, each out of rhythm with the others. A woman stands behind a counter, her hair in two coiled braids. When I show her the letter, she says nothing but points to two metal chairs.

As I sit in that cold-backed chair, I fold and unfold my hands. The clock says one minute to ten. Then ten. Then past ten. Like Janosik, I'm about to be racked and tortured.

I wonder what Adam Uherco does all day. I wonder if he's now slobbering and screaming along with the others.

Just as I'm thinking that we must have come on the wrong day, a policeman in a blue uniform enters. Epaulets on the shoulders, stripes on the pockets. Tati and I both stand, but the policeman gestures for Tati to sit back down. I'm to go in alone.

In the inner office, the Russian flag hangs limp in a corner. A second policeman with more stripes, and even a few pins, sits behind a wooden desk. The first officer goes to stand next to him, hands clasped behind his back.

For me, they've provided another metal chair. There's the tick of the clock in here, the rattling crowd of typewriters out there.

The policeman with the pins and extra stripes opens a file. I glimpse my name. The papers flutter as he sorts through them — have they really written so much about me? Babicak must have been true to his word. The policeman holds up a photograph.

I tilt forward to see that it's of the parade. But not just the parade — it's of me, too. My heart churns faster. There I am, holding a lighter to the flag.

"Is this you?" the policeman asks. His voice is surprisingly high, almost like a girl's.

"It is, sir."

"You don't deny the charges, then?"

"No, sir." Though I don't know what the charges are, I won't be a smart aleck. Not here.

"You are charged with treachery against the regime."

I suck in my breath. All I did was touch a flame to a piece of cloth. The typewriters rack a jangle of noise.

"If you were not a schoolboy, such a serious offense would result in years of hard labor. Since you are but a student, we will be more lenient."

Out the high window, a bird begins to sing. I hear smaller birds. There must be a nest. Adam Uherco was also a student.

The policeman writes something, then shuts my file. He picks a bit of lint off his sleeve before saying in his high, thin voice, "Since this year of school is almost over, you will finish it. But in the fall, you will go to a different kind of school."

"I beg your pardon, sir?" I cannot have heard him right. The birds. The typewriter. The ticking of the clock have all interfered with my hearing.

"You will apprentice to be a miner, Mr. Chrobak."

A miner. But that's crazy. I grip the arms of my metal chair. It's not the insane asylum, but the mines are almost as bad. "I want to be a doctor. Maybe even a psychiatrist, like my father." Becoming a doctor is a new idea. But suddenly it seems perfectly logical.

The standing policeman shifts from one foot to the other.

The seated one clears his throat. "That's no longer in the cards for you, Mr. Chrobak."

A miner. Karel and I once visited a cave called the Wicked Hole. As a joke, we blew out our lanterns. Darkness swallowed us. The mountain swallowed us. There was no way out. Suffocating on blackness, I scrambled and fell. Scrambled and fell.

I think of how miners emerge from deep within the earth, covered in black dust, headlamps tied to their foreheads.

I could never be a miner.

I'd rather be a janitor.

I'd rather pump gas.

"That's it," the policeman says. "You are dismissed."

I go out, and they call in my father. Sitting in the chair again, I try to be courageous and undaunted like Janosik.

And then I think of Dr. Machovik, our own doctor and friend, he who's invited us year after year to his vacation house in the pines. I think of how our friendly Dr. Machovik works just down the hall.

At last the policeman shoos Tati out and smacks the door shut behind him. Tati's eyes are dark sockets. Without a word, he beckons to me.

Going down the hall, past the sweeping janitor, we say nothing. Nor do we speak on the walk to the bus stop, rain showering over us. Nor do we utter a word on the bus. On the street beside us, a Gypsy wagon passes, the horse's head bent down in the rain. Maybe I could become a Gypsy. I could dye my hair black and run away. I could get myself stolen.

We silently pass the men with the walkie-talkies. As we walk to our building and up inside it, my lips are sealed.

Only when we're back in our apartment, the door firmly bolted, do I turn to Tati and say, "We have to get out."

He nods. "I know."

I look out the window to see the rain falling hard,

120

pummeling the tulips along the path. I've already gotten soaked this morning. So I ask Tati if I can stay home
from school.

"You might as well."

Then he gathers his briefcase and his umbrella with
the curved bone handle. He reties his dark-blue tie and
is out the door.

Standing at my window, I watch him go down
the path between the wet tulips, holding the black
umbrella, a shield against all bad things falling from
the sky.

When he turns the corner, we're both alone.

Why Is Tati So Late?

That evening, Bela and I spoon down cabbage soup flavored with smoked sausage. Mami paces. She's so upset about my becoming a miner that she doesn't say a thing about my reading a Janosik comic at the table.

When the soup grows cold and there's still no sign of Tati, Mami sets the pot on the stove and covers it with a lid.

The three of us go to the couch, but none of us flicks on the television.

"Why is Tati so late?" Bela wants to know.

"Shhh," Mami says, urging Bela's head onto her lap. "Sleep now, dear heart." Stroking Bela's yellow hair, she sings a lullaby about little birds going to a nest. When Bela falls asleep, Mami carries her to bed.

I turn off the lights and go to the window, scanning the blackness outside. I'm looking for the two policemen. For the man with the beige hair in his VW Beetle. For the men with the walkie-talkies. For who knows who.

Maybe everyone will go away now that my punishment has been assigned.

I think again of being locked inside of black caves.

When Mami comes back, I switch the lights on and see that her cheeks are streaked with tears. She sinks down beside me. "What's going to happen to us, Patrik? What, what, what?" She shoves back the hair along her temples.

"Don't get so upset. His bus is just running behind." What does Mami expect *me* to do? I can't bring Tati home.

"I don't mean just your father. I mean you, too."

At that, I shut my mouth.

The clock ticks on, as if the world were still nicely ordered. The cuckoo bird slides in and out, pecking the hour. But my heart pecks unevenly, like the real pigeons on the window ledge. What if something really *has* happened this time?

At the sound of footsteps on the stairs, Mami dries her eyes on her sleeve. She jumps up and swings the door open wide. "Rumer?" She calls down.

"Klaudia," he replies.

When Tati comes in, his face is as white as a sheet of paper. He isn't carrying his briefcase. His hair is grayer than in the morning. "They planted anti-Communist literature in my desk," he says. "They claim my office radio was tuned to Voice of America."

He flops down on the couch. "They interviewed me all day."

"We have to get out of here," Mami whispers, looking at the window.

I look, too.

"They ransacked my files. They've even forbidden me to carry my briefcase, saying I might steal state secrets."

"What will they do to you?"

He takes one of Mami's carefully ironed doilies and crumples it in his fist, saying, "If they sent me to do road-work up at Prikra, that would be a light sentence. Now I may end up in prison. Stitching Soviet flags all day."

Mami starts to cry again.

"What will we do?" I ask.

"We have to get out. For Patrik's sake. For mine." Tati gets up, crosses the room, and tugs the curtains closed. "The whole time they grilled me, I was planning."

"And?" Mami asks.

"We will pretend to go to Yugoslavia on vacation," Tati says, sitting back down.

I pull up a chair. "And from there?" I ask. Yugoslavia is still a Communist country. It's still in the Soviet Bloc.

"We'll go to Trieste, Italy. It's across the water. We'll need a boat."

"How will we get money for something like that?" Mami straightens a lamp shade. The shade rocks off balance, and she straightens it again.

"When I published that paper in West Germany," Tati says, "I was paid in Western currency. The hospital still has the money in my account."

"So the boat can be bought," says Mami, sitting down beside Tati, the couch dipping with her weight. "But we still need permission to go to Yugoslavia. Will they give us that? Will they permit us to leave for vacation?"

Leaning his forearms across his knees, Tati clasps his hands tightly and sighs. He jiggles his folded hands up and down.

A few years ago, we went camping in Yugoslavia. I remember the border with its brown-uniformed guards. I remember driving down by the giant mirror of Lake Balaton, the little hotel that smelled like old rain and had a portrait of the Hungarian president

125

hung too high. Then we crossed the next border and came to a town on the cliff, with donkey carts and bougainvillea and a bust of Lenin in the square. We finally arrived at the campground of towering trees, tents under the trees, and a half-moon of beach.

As I'm about to change into my pajamas, I notice something white hanging outside my open window. Could it be? Yes, it's a note from Danika, the first since Bozek came along. Maybe she's changed her mind about me. With my heart beating like Ringo Starr's drums, I reel in the scrap of paper.

Unfolding the square, my fingers tremble. My vision trembles across the words. But the note reads: *I heard you got called to the police station.*

How did Danika learn this? Who spread the news? I smash up the paper and throw it on the floor.

But then I pick up the note and smooth it out. Maybe she doesn't really care about the stupid police. Maybe she's trying to be friendly. Maybe things aren't working out with Bozek.

But this is obviously no love note. Danika is just being nosy. I consider writing something rude back, like *None of your business.*

A small voice tells me to be careful. In the end,

Janosik was betrayed by his sweetheart. When she fell in love with another, she craftily destroyed his three gifts. First she destroyed his magical staff. Then she destroyed his magical shirt and his magical belt. She left him defenseless.

Danika's violin music begins to wander into my bedroom. Vivaldi winds through the air like vines.

I take a box of matches from my drawer. Lighting one, I hold the tiny flame to the edge of Danika's note.

Cherub Pee

In history class, Mr. Noll surveys me over the top of his glasses. What does he know? Maybe he's a spy for Babicak, on a mission to get me to miner school right away. I imagine the news spreading from the police station in all directions, like the ripples from a rock thrown into a pond.

As Libena reads aloud, I gaze at the page, the words a blur. It no longer matters if I memorize dates or battles. Come fall, there will be no more Peloponnesian Wars for me. Instead I'll be learning to sling a pickax alongside other boys who torched the flag.

In botany class, Mrs. Jakim now suspects me of sending bottle caps instead of coins to the poor Cubans. Come fall, there will be no more Bazima Forest for me, no more identifying trees. I'll be on field trips under the earth, identifying veins of ore.

As a miner, I may not be allowed to have a camera. I might not even want one. Working so hard, I might not care about taking pictures.

During marching drill in the gymnasium, I watch out for knowing looks. *Patrik Chrobak, the future miner.* Ha, ha.

As Danika passes me, going the other way with knees lifted high, she raises her eyebrows at me inquiringly.

I meet her bright-blue eyes, then turn away. Her father must have told her about me. Who has *she* told? By now surely Bozek knows.

After school, I invite Karel and Emil to join me in the shade of the nearby clump of trees.

"I have something to tell you," I say, picking up a stick. "Something you probably already know."

They glance at each other, then both shrug. Karel holds out his hands, palms up.

"Spit it out," says Emil.

So, doodling in the dirt with my stick, pushing aside bits of trash, I tell all about my summons, the interrogation, and how I'm to become a miner.

They listen, Karel with an open mouth, both giving astonished grunts.

At the end, I draw a big *X* in the dirt, saying, "So that's that. That's the story."

Emil puts his foot squarely on the *X*. "They say the workers of the world should throw off their chains," he says. "But now they'll put *you* in chains."

There's a silence, long and deep, until Karel says, "Guess we won't see you around next year."

"Guess not." I throw down the stick and lean back against a tree trunk. "Guess not."

"Do you want to take the Beatles single for a while?" Emil asks, pulling a cigarette from his satchel.

"Thanks, but no. I don't have a record player."

"Plus Patrik can't risk getting caught with something like a record," Karel says.

I look upon my band of loyal men—Emil striking a match, Karel doodling with the stick I threw down. Like Janosik, I won't take this lying down. "My father and I are going to Bratislava tomorrow to pick up a boat," I tell them. "We're going to Yugoslavia."

"You're going on vacation at a time like this?" Karel asks.

I don't say a single word. A long look is enough.

Emil moves the flame toward his cigarette, then stops. "Oh," he says, letting the match burn out.

"I get it," Karel says.

"This may be our only real good-bye," I say.

Emil puts the cigarette into his pocket and tucks it safely out of sight, taking longer than he needs to. Then he holds out his hand, palm down. Karel places his on top, and I put my hand over Karel's. Three layers of our hands. This used to be our ritual before going into battle for Janosik. Under my palm, I feel the pulsing warmth of Karel's skin. "I'll write to you guys," I say. "I'll find a way."

"Sure," says Emil.

"Sure thing," says Karel.

But we all know that mail is a very iffy proposition between America and here.

After I leave them, I wander through Cherub Pee Park, moving toward the exact spot where Danika told me no. Shadows shift across the flagstones, and I think again of being a miner. Most of my life will be spent underground, in darkness. I'll enjoy this kind of sunshine only on weekends. If there are weekends. . . .

Then I look up and see them. Sitting on the fountain where Danika and I sat. But instead of having a confusing conversation, they're kissing. Bozek has one hand on Danika's smooth cheek. Behind them, the stone cherub pees on and on without stopping.

My heart pedals furiously. Forward. Backward. I want to run away, pretend I've seen nothing. I want to run toward them, tear them away from each other.

I march across the flagstones, scattering a group of ducks. My shadow falls across the love of my life and this . . . this thief. Their arms drop and they stare up at me, blinking.

"What is it, Patrik?" Danika asks. "You look so . . ."

I interrupt her: "You know what it is."

She turns her face away from Bozek. *The police station?* she mouths silently, exaggerating the words.

Bozek knits his eyebrows and tugs on his red scarf.

I step closer, my heart tumbling in circles. "I've loved you all my life. That's what." I bite the inside of my cheek, forbidding myself to cry.

"Oh!" Danika says, her voice breathy.

I want to seize her, press my lips to hers.

Bozek scuffs at a weed with the tip of his shoe. "I didn't know. . . . I had no idea. . . ."

"You didn't know that Danika and I were practically sweethearts before you came along? If you'd never come to Trencin, we'd be fine!" I glare at the cherub.

"Patrik!" Danika cries.

Bozek takes her hand and grips it hard. "You said that you and Patrik were good friends. Very good friends. But that was all."

The skin by Danika's left eye twitches.

"You got Danika interested in the party so she'd like you better," I accuse.

"Me?" Bozek touches his chest with one fingertip. He stands up, shielding his eyes against the lowering sun. I see that his American jeans are a little too short. "That had nothing to do with *me*. Danika's father was already set to join."

I sit down on the edge of a fountain, away from Danika. Away from both of them. Bozek is right. I lean my elbows on my legs and drop my head.

In the long pause, the ducks return, lowering their beaks to nibble the grass.

"I'm going to become a miner," I suddenly blurt out. I don't mean to say this — the words just come.

Danika asks, "What, Patrik? What did you say?"

"Next year I'm going to a different school. To become an apprentice."

"A miner school?"

"Was that your idea?" Bozek asks.

"Yes, and of course not."

Awkwardly, Danika slides closer to me, the fabric of her skirt catching on the stone fountain. "Tell me this isn't true, Patrik. Tell me you're just joking."

"It's . . ." Now I can't help the tears. Like the words, they flow out of me. I wipe my eyes on my sleeves. "You already knew." I manage at last.

"Of course I didn't," she says, shaking her head. "I knew about the police station but not the rest. How would I?"

"From your father."

She looks puzzled, then shakes her head again. "He didn't tell me."

"A miner. That's a bummer," says Bozek softly. "A real bummer."

Danika moves still nearer. Placing her hand over mine, she says, "I didn't think . . ."

"You didn't think the party would send kids to be miners? Is that it? You didn't think . . ." I stand up and the ducks take off, beating the air with their brown wings.

The Fancy Free

As Tati and I leave for Bratislava, towing a trailer that used to be a farm cart, the men with the walkie-talkies patrol the street in front of our building. This time, Danika's father is out there, too, and they're all talking together.

"Who are those men?" Tati asks.

"They've been watching us."

"Why is Mr. Holub with them?" he asks, peering into the rearview mirror.

"Dunno. . . ."

Tati drums his fingers on the steering wheel. But the men make no move to follow us. Even when we drive out of town, no one chases us down. No one stops us. The flat two-lane road of the countryside begins to wind through villages, then past enormous collective farms. I roll down the window and take a deep breath of the river grasses. Soon I won't see this again. I'll be far away. Where, I don't know.

When we camped in Yugoslavia, I met a boy my age who was also vacationing there from Czechoslovakia. His family had a bright-red boat called the *Wave Rider*. We rode bikes together and skipped stones across the water toward Italy. One morning, the Yugoslav patrol boats raced toward shore, white foam frothing behind them. They were bringing in the *Wave Rider*. Alexej and his family sat with bowed heads, two uniformed Yugoslav guards at the helm.

"*Alexej!*" I called out.

He didn't look at me. In fact, he turned his head away. The *Wave Rider* scraped the cement ramp. One by one, each member of the family got out, wading the last few feet: the father and mother, Alexej and his two little brothers. Flecks of red paint drifted in the water.

Without a word, the guards handcuffed the parents. Then they marched the whole family — those of us watching had to step aside — to a police van puffing tailpipe exhaust.

* * *

At noon, Tati stops the car to eat the picnic lunch Mami packed. There's cold sausage, some bread, a tomato and pear for each of us. In the distance, the Bratislava castle rises above the city. Unlike ours in Trencin, it doesn't teeter on a precipice, but perches comfortably on its hilltop.

I watch the cars on the road. A dirty white VW goes by. I squint, looking for rust.

"Let's fetch our boat, Patrik," says Tati as we finish up. "Let's get it over with." He lifts the lid of the picnic basket, and we pack everything back in.

We enter the town and drive through the steep gray canyons of Soviet apartment buildings.

"See how the statues of Stalin are all gone?" Tati asks.

"Guess so. I never saw them."

"Ever since he killed millions of people after the Second World War, he's been pretty unpopular." Tati laughs, but not as if he thinks anything is funny.

There are still plenty of Lenin statues. All waiting to be pissed upon.

Red-painted slogans scream: *Workers of the World, Unite!* and *Down with the Bourgeoisie!* There's also a small handwritten scrawl: *Freedom from the Russian occupation. Now!*

Finally we drive into the old medieval town, with its pale tan buildings and soft curving walls. The flags of Russia and Czechoslovakia hang from the buildings. I hold up my camera and pretend to shoot photos, though I'm still out of film. Maybe Tati will stop so I can buy some. But later. Right now we have to get the boat.

I look for signs of all that Bozek brags about, but see only a tattered poster advertising a local band. I spot just one man wearing blue jeans.

Tati consults his handwritten directions to the state-run store, the *tuzex*. He hands me the slip of paper, and, as he drives, I read aloud: "'Left here, go straight, look for the gas station on the corner.'"

Another white VW. But that means nothing. Beetles are everywhere. I see a blue one. A brown one.

At last we arrive. The *tuzex* is a plain, flat-looking storefront with small windows. Tati parks the car and trailer, and we walk up to the entrance.

A small man with very red lips sits blocking the doorway. When our shadows fall across him, he looks up. "What are you here to buy?" he asks Tati.

"A fiberglass boat. I called ahead to order it."

"The purpose of this boat?" The man purses his lips.

I fasten the bottom button of my shirt.

"It's just for recreation," Tati answers. "My family is going on vacation."

"And where are your *bon*s for such a big purchase?"

Tati takes out his wallet and displays the special currency inside.

"And where did you get so many *bon*s?"

From the inside pocket of his jacket, Tati takes the letter from the hospital. He unfolds it carefully and hands it to the man.

The man purses his lips again, reading about the paper published in the West. At last he reluctantly waves us inside.

We enter into a heaven. The store is filled with fragrant coffees, gold-wrapped chocolates, imported cheeses, and nice clothes. While Tati goes into the little office in the back, I examine the reel-to-reel tape recorders. I look at the transistor radios that have all been fixed in the factory to prevent anyone from getting the Voice of America.

I look at the recorders again, running my fingertip over the big spools of brown recording tape. With one of these, I could record Emil's Beatles music for myself. What is taking Tati so long? Is there a problem? Maybe there's no boat available. Maybe it's like my film. No boat to be found. Maybe we've come all this way for nothing.

Or maybe someone has discovered the real reason Tati wants the boat.

I walk back over to the radios, examining them as if I were a serious buyer. In Yugoslavia we'll pretend to be just normal campers, like we were before. We'll take our boat out every day, as if for fun. We'll make campfires and gaze at the distant freedom of Italy, straining to make out the lights on the shore.

When we camped there, a woman set out swimming. She was towing her little daughter in an inner tube. The two got smaller and smaller until we couldn't see them at all, even with binoculars. We never saw either of them again.

Tati finally does return, flourishing a piece of tan paper. It says he has paid for a boat and gives the Bratislava address where we are to get it. Beside the address, the man in the office has scribbled directions.

Back in the car, I again read off directions while Tati drives: "'Right here, around the bend . . .'"

We pass a little store that might sell film, but I say nothing.

Finally we arrive outside town at a big parking lot.

Beyond the barbed-wire fence, I see cars, trucks, boats, and trailers.

At the guard hut, a soldier looks over Tati's tan paper. Then he picks up the phone.

"Who's he calling?" I whisper to Tati.

"Probably the *tuzex*. To make sure we didn't counterfeit the bill of sale."

The man comes out, climbs into our backseat, and instructs: "Go on through the gate. . . . Turn here. . . . Now here."

The trailer bumps along behind, clattering over the rutty dirt lot.

Finally, we pull up beside a turquoise boat, gleaming with newness. There's a name painted along the side: *The Fancy Free*. The name makes me smile.

The three of us climb out, banging shut the Fiat's doors.

While Tati and the soldier look back and forth between the paperwork and the boat itself, I stroke the hull's glossy surface. I pat the bulk of the East German engine.

"We're going on a trip to Yugoslavia," Tati explains to the soldier.

Even now, if this man were to have suspicions, he could just call someone. The boat's name suddenly seems to give everything away. It's as if someone gave us a boat with this name on purpose.

"Here, Patrik, help me," Tati says.

We winch the boat onto the trailer, the soldier helping. We secure it on with long cables.

When we drop the soldier at his hut, we all shake hands. And then we are out the gate with our prize.

"The name!" I say when we're back on the road.

Tati slaps the steering wheel and laughs.

"It's not funny," I say. "Do you think that soldier guessed?"

"Who knows?" Tati glances in the rearview mirror. As he drives, I feel the tug of the boat behind us.

This time I see the car for sure. I see the rust.

On that half-moon of beach, we'll have to watch out for that car. We'll have to watch out for the Yugoslav patrol boats flying their red-white-and-blue flags. We'll have to be careful of even fellow campers. On the final morning we'll have to leave early, before the afternoon thunderstorms scroll along the horizon.

"What about the travel permission?" I ask Tati.

He sighs and taps the steering wheel, saying, "One thing at a time, Patrik."

In the past, whenever we traveled out of the country for vacation, Tati went to the downtown office and got travel papers. But he won't be able to do that anymore. Without that slip of paper, the Czech guards at the border will turn us back. This journey to fetch the boat will be all for nothing.

Tati taps the steering wheel again, accidentally honking the horn. "Things will work out."

But things might not work out. We may never leave. Someone may figure out what we're up to.

At that point, would they send soldiers or only police? Would we hear sirens?

If only I were old enough to take charge, even in a small way. "How about letting me drive, Tati?"

"*You?* But you've never . . ."

"I want to try. This is as good a time as any."

"But the boat . . ." he protests. Yet, at the spot where we stopped for lunch, Tati pulls off the road. He gets out, gesturing for me to switch places with him. The motor is still running.

I've sat behind the wheel of a car before, but never with the engine turned on. I don't know what to do with my arms and legs.

"Push in the clutch, and move the gearshift forward and toward you," Tati instructs.

I do as he says, and the Fiat lurches.

"Take it easy."

I move the car onto the road, into the golden late afternoon. We're almost the only travelers headed for Trencin. This may be the last time we'll drive into town from Bratislava. The last time I'll see these canvas-backed trucks trudging along the farm roads, the row of neat white houses, the cows grazing against the factory smokestacks.

But these thoughts are mere whispers. Mostly I'm focused on gripping the hard plastic steering wheel with the ridges that fit my fingers. I'm gauging the pressure of my foot on the pedal, focused on not hitting that donkey cart with its load of vegetables. As I take the curve just right, our boat rattling behind, a delicious feeling of power surges through me. I'm bringing home *The Fancy Free* for all of us. If only we could snatch up Mami and Bela, if only I could drive us all the way to America . . .

On our final morning in the campground, Tati and I will go early to the store to buy extra gas. Mami will pack a normal picnic — nothing extra to arouse suspicion. We won't tell blabbermouth Bela a thing. The sky will be clear, the olive-green horizon of Italy beckoning like a promise.

Leave Us Alone

On the outskirts of Trencin, Tati takes the wheel again, saying, "Nice work, son. You're a good driver." Just then, we pass a police motorcycle parked by the side of the road.

As we go by, the motorcycle roars into action. The siren sounds: *Wawawa!*

Swearing, Tati pulls over, bringing the boat to a bumpy halt.

I clutch the armrest.

The officer comes to the window, the pistol on his waist at eye level. Reaching out a meaty hand, he asks to see Tati's driver's license. Studying the license, he asks, "Where did you get such a new boat, Mr. Chrobak?"

"It's *Doctor*. Dr. Chrobak."

"Doctor, then. Please answer my question, Doctor."

"I bought it in Bratislava. The bill of sale is right here." Tati opens the glove compartment and pulls out the tan paper.

After the policeman looks at the paper, he disappears, going back to the boat. Out the side window, I see him kick the trailer tires. Once he sees the name, we'll be done for.

Finally, the officer returns to the window. He hands back Tati's license and the bill of sale. "All seems to be in order, Mr. Chrobak. You are free to go."

Tati eases back onto the road, muttering, "Close call."

"What could he have done?" I hold my thumb on my wrist, feeling the thud of pulse.

"Depends on how tight the net is."

"They've cast a net?" My pulse beats harder.

"Only time will tell," Tati says slowly.

I think of Mr. Holub talking to the walkie-talkie men. That's the net. That's how it's cast.

I think again of my future in the dark cave. My headlamp may go out. Smothering on darkness, I'll have no batteries. I'll have to scramble to find the way. Scramble and fall. I'll batter my way with the pickax.

Tati drives to the parking lot, where he lines the boat up next to a pole. "Stay here," he says. "I'll be right back."

I get out and lean against the Fiat. In the dusky light, I make out Danika headed toward me. This is the first time we've been alone since she came to my darkroom looking for the photo of herself with Bozek.

Her eyes grow round at the sight of the boat. "Is this *yours*?"

I nod, my heart rolling loose.

"What's it for?"

"A trip to Yugoslavia."

"Isn't it early to go on vacation? School isn't out for a long time."

I shrug. "My father wants to go before the summer crowds."

"*The Fancy Free,*" she says, tracing the script with her fingertip. "That's a nice name."

A name that gives it all away.

"My father let me drive," I tell her.

Her eyes widen again. "All by yourself?"

"Of course. It was easy."

Her eyes brighten. Probably even Bozek hasn't driven a car with a boat in tow.

Tati returns with cables and two padlocks. We tie the boat to the pole, Danika threading a cable through the metal rings.

When the boat is secured, Tati goes inside, leaving Danika and me behind. The lights in the parking lot come on, turning the air from gray to orange. The nighttime crickets begin to whir.

"I have something to tell you," Danika says. She edges close and I flinch at her familiar scent. She pauses, then says, "My father joined."

It's like a padlock snapping shut. "Fantastic. That's fantastic news."

"I know you don't approve, Patrik. I know"—she drops her voice—"that your family isn't pro-party. But just think what this will mean for *my* family." Her gaze outlines our escape vessel. "I thought you should know."

"Okay. You've done your duty. Now I know." I lean against the boat's revealing name. "I ask just one thing, Danika. Leave us alone. Leave my family alone."

"Why, Patrik, I'd never . . ."

"The damage is done. Just imagine me working deep under the dark ground."

She passes one hand over her forehead, saying, "My father had nothing to do with that."

"Save it," I mutter, striding away.

Upstairs, Tati has folded up the tan bill of sale and is tucking it into his wallet. Mami busily smoothes the doilies on the arms of the chairs. Bela plays with her doll, the miniature furniture made of boxes strewn across the floor.

I approach Tati, pulling up a chair until it rests arm to arm with his. I place my hand over the doily. I feel the neat pattern against my palm, then whisper, "We have to be careful. Mr. Holub has joined the party."

Tati shuts his wallet, grips it with both hands. "How long have you known this, Patrik?"

"I just learned." Which is not technically a lie.

Mami begins to straighten the doilies all over again.

"What are we going to do?" I ask. Already shadows are crisscrossing the windows.

Tati slaps the wallet against his open palm. "We'll have to leave very soon," he says. "We'll begin preparations."

"Can't we go right away?"

"We're not even packed, Patrik. There are matters to be attended to."

"Like the travel permission."

"Exactly."

"And what other matters?"

"There are some patients I have to see."

"Patients?" How could any patient be in worse shape than we are?

"And I have an important meeting the day after tomorrow."

On the day we leave for Italy, it will be way too late. The waves will be choppy, the wind stiff. Clouds will be bunched along the Italian horizon, purple and mean. Two patrol boats will circle the water, the wind slapping their flags.

Suddenly, the wind will pick up. It'll hurtle the storm toward us, the waves rearing higher. All the other boats will head for shore.

But we'll aim for Italy, storm or no storm.

With rain falling in drops the size of coins, the patrol boats will gain on us. The guards will stand up, waving their arms, roaring a stream of threats and outrage through their megaphones.

I go to my room and lie down on the bed that is right below Danika's. The smell of developing fluids eases through the closet door. Outside, the men with the walkie-talkies are probably nosing around *The Fancy Free,* noting the giveaway name. Before they put two and two together, we have to get away. Only one small piece of paper keeps us here.

Bunnies and Vegetables

After school, I ride the bus to the square building that houses the Trencin police. Men peer at me from the blackened windows of the vans. Yet in spite of that, I mount the slick white stairs and pull open the heavy door.

I go down the tall-ceilinged hallways where the paint is still peeling, the janitor still sweeping. I head right to the dreaded 129, where the counter woman still wears her hair in two coiled braids.

"Excuse me, madam," I say, hoisting my book satchel from one shoulder to the other. "I'm looking for Dr. Jakub Machovik."

She eyes me as if she recognizes my face but can't remember from where.

"He's my doctor. For years and years. At least he used to be."

She opens a binder, runs her finger down a type-written list of names, shakes her head.

"He's new. He just came here recently."

With a sigh, she reaches for a thinner binder. The list is shorter, and her finger stops right away. "Room 151," she says.

Out in the hallway, I take the turn I saw Machovik take. From there I come to 151.

Staring at the door, I try to comfort myself by thinking of the basket of newborn bunnies. I try to remember if Dr. Machovik himself acted kindly toward them or whether that was just his wife.

But thinking of small, helpless bunnies is a bad idea. I raise my fist and knock.

No one answers. Maybe the doctor has seen me through the frosted glass and is lying low.

I sit down on the floor and pull my schoolbooks from the satchel. First I do some geometry, completing five proofs. Then I read a little of Franz Kafka, who wrote about dead ends like this one. When the janitor comes by, I have to stand so he can sweep beneath me. When he's gone, I sit back down.

Hours pass. But if I don't wait here, we'll get turned

back at the first border and I'll become a miner, inching my way through black caves. Up and down the hallway, I hear keys turning in locks.

At last Dr. Machovik comes around the corner. Seeing me there on the floor, he stops. Then he approaches, stroking his goatee. "Why, Patrik," he says. "What a surprise." He strokes his goatee some more. "To what do I owe this visit?"

"I have a sore throat."

"A sore throat, eh? You don't have a new doctor?"

"No one I trust," I say, then lay it on thick. "No one like you."

He reaches into his jacket pocket, pulls out a key, and opens the door. He gestures me into this lair, where there's a desk, a red flag stretched across the wall, a picture of Mrs. Machovik in a silver frame.

"I have none of my instruments here, of course." He waves toward a stack of papers. "But I might as well take a quick look. Come over to the window."

I go to where the late-afternoon light falls.

"You've gotten too tall for me." Dr. Machovik scoots a chair into the light. After I've obediently sat, he pulls down my lower jaw and peers in. "Please say *ahh* for me."

Just like olden times, I open wide.

After a moment, he says, "I don't see any redness."

"Hmm, that's strange. It still hurts." I swallow hard for emphasis.

"Drink lots of water. Take an aspirin."

So that's that. I have no further reason to be here. But I didn't wait hours to have my throat looked at. Folding my arms across my chest, I say, "My father is working hard lately, Doctor. I'm worried about him. He needs a vacation."

Dr. Machovik leans back against his desk. "He could go to my house by the river."

"He needs to go somewhere for longer than a weekend," I say, proceeding as though through high grass. "We've bought a boat, in fact. We want to go to Yugoslavia."

"A lovely place indeed."

I go through a landscape of prickles and thorns. "It's the travel permission, Dr. Machovik. I thought I could save my father some trouble by getting it myself. From you. I know you have a different job now, you see. . . ."

He shakes his head ever so slightly, traces the outline of a floor tile with the tip of his shoe. "That's not my job."

In the silence I hear another key turning in a lock.

I have come for nothing. Waited for nothing. Exposed us for nothing.

I must step into even deeper peril. "How is your vegetable garden?" I ask.

"Very well. Things are ripening nicely."

"Are your neighbors still enjoying their share?"

Dr. Machovik narrows his eyes. "I don't . . . don't share with them."

"Oh?" I act surprised. "Not anymore?"

Silence again.

Now I am certainly done for. Dr. Machovik will have me arrested.

He pulls hard on his goatee. He looks at the ceiling, where a long strip of paint is about to drift loose.

Yet I don't budge from my spot in the light from the window. "How are the bunnies?" I ask.

Dr. Machovik frowns at first, as if he doesn't remember the bunnies, then says, "Ah, yes. They're all grown up. Already released to the wild."

He looks to the ceiling again, one corner of his mouth twitching.

I don't move. I don't give up.

At last Dr. Machovik clears this throat and says, "I suppose I could arrange travel papers. Just this once."

Turning his back to me, he lifts the receiver of the black phone and dials. I hear the *ring ring* on the other end. A voice answers, and Dr. Machovik says something very softly.

Facing me again, he says, "Go to 129 and the secretary will have your papers for you. I think"—he looks up from under his eyebrows—"you already know where room 129 is."

As I go past the walkie-talkie men on our corner, I wonder if they're aware of what I carry tucked deep in my satchel. I wonder how wide the net is cast.

When I climb the stairs to the apartment, Mami calls down, "Patrik! Is that you?" I recognize the high-strung voice she uses whenever Tati keeps her waiting.

I come in to find both my parents on their feet, as if they've been pacing. The empty dinner plates sit on the table, reflecting the glow of the swinging lamp above.

"Where have you been?" Mami asks. She's still wearing her nurse's cap.

I rummage in my satchel until I slip the envelope from between the pages of my history book. I hold up the prize, saying, "Guess what I have!"

"Not more bad news," Tati says. "I hope. . . ."

"Not at all." I toss the envelope onto the table.

Tati opens it, pulls out the document. Mami leans close and they both study what's written. "How?" Tati manages.

"I got it from Dr. Machovik. Remember when we saw him at the police station?"

"You got this from *him*?" Tati sits down under the swinging lamp of the dining table, bumping a plate with his elbow.

"Aren't you happy? I expected you to be happy."

"Everything is now much more complicated— that's all," says Tati.

I know what he means, but I push on. "Complicated? What's complicated? We have travel papers, and we can go."

"But now Dr. Machovik knows. . . ." Tati says gloomily.

"Do you think he'll turn us in?" Mami asks.

"He can't," I say, bragging. "I brought up how he doesn't report all his vegetables."

Tati plunges his head into his hands.

"But the papers are legitimate, aren't they?" Mami asks. "They have the right seal, don't they?"

"Of course they're legitimate." I turn to her. "I went there all by myself and got them. And now no one even thanks me. You"—I twist back to Tati—"weren't going to do anything about travel papers. Nothing at all."

Tati drops his hands and looks up at me. He runs his eyes from my face down to my shoes, and back up again. At last he says, "I'm sorry, Patrik. Come here." He jerks a chair close.

I sit. Across the table, Mami is tucking the travel papers neatly into the envelope. From the bedroom, I hear Bela's tiny voice call out, "I can't sleep, Mami!"

Mami gets up and puts the envelope on a shelf in the china cabinet. When she's gone out and the soft sound of a lullaby emerges from the other room, Tati says, "I don't know what's wrong with me lately. I feel like my feet are stuck in cement."

"Are you afraid to leave?"

"Of course I am. I have no idea what I'll do in America," he says. "I won't be able to work as a doctor. I don't know how I'll make money."

I study Tati. It seems that his hair is grayer than just a few days ago. For the first time, I notice his small chin, a sign, they say, of weakness. But he has a good point. What *would* he do in America? Suddenly I wonder if he'd become a miner.

"I can help. I can work."

Tati smiles. He pats my hand. "That may be fine eventually, Patrik. But we have no money to travel with. We have nothing to live on once I abandon my job."

"Your aunt . . ." I say, but then remember that the gas station is shut down. We can't even pump gas.

Eighty-four Dollars

"We have to pack," I tell Mami the next morning. "We have to get ready."

"But your father hasn't . . ." she says, turning from the sink, which is full of dishes.

I cut in. "Tati is still busy with his patients. It's up to us."

"Patrik," Mami says, laying a soapy hand on my arm, "I, too, feel bad about leaving my patients. I, too, don't know what I'll do in America."

"You'll find something. I'll help you find something. . . ."

"You're a sweet boy, Patrik." Mami draws me into her arms, the way she hasn't done since I was little. Her hands are damp on the back of my shirt. I look down at the top of her head, then lay my cheek against it.

Abruptly, she releases me and runs her hands down the front of her apron. "You're right, Patrik. We'd better pack."

I sit down on the sofa. I hadn't thought of Mami's life, her work at the clinic. The way she might not have nursing work in America. The way she might not be able to do what she loves. She might have to become an American janitor. Staring at the dust motes, at the windows where the tiny spy microphones may be hidden, I suddenly feel as paralyzed as Tati.

After a while, I make myself get up. I go to the hall closet and pull out the suitcases, then carry two into Mami and Tati's bedroom, the smallest into Bela's room, and the last one to mine. I pack a few clothes, using the shirts and shorts as padding for my camera. I slip my photos — including those of Danika — between pieces of cardboard. I open the door to my darkroom and gaze inside. In America there won't be money for all these chemicals.

I hear Mami saying to Bela, "Just the summer clothes, darling. Just the camping clothes."

It may get cold in Scranton, Pennsylvania. Without money, how will we buy winter clothes? Shivering, we may long for these coats and scarves and mittens we're leaving behind.

I listen for the phone to ring. Or for a knock on the door. How do arrests happen? Would they send one man to get us? Or two or three? Would they send the men with the walkie-talkies, or the beige man in his VW?

Has Dr. Machovik alerted someone?

When I lift Tati's framed medical diploma off the wall, Mami objects. "If we're caught with that," she says, "they'll know we're planning to go for good. The game will be up."

I hang the diploma back on the nail. I take a step away and stare at the glass rectangle, then move forward to straighten the frame. "And *you'll* have to leave behind those silver candlesticks," I tell Mami.

Looking as if she'll cry, she puts the candlesticks back in the cupboard. She shuts the glass door with a tiny *thunk*.

Soon we'll disappear, never to return. Then people like the men on the corner will stroll through our apartment with their polished shoes, helping themselves to things that cannot be bought even on the black market.

After a while, I wonder why we're packing anything at all. We've got the boat. We've got the travel permission. We should just head out. Right now. If only Tati would agree.

When Tati comes home, Mami brings down the china teapot from the top shelf. She pulls out a roll of green American money. It's all in ones and fives, left here by the Pennsylvania relatives during a visit. When I was little, I studied the faces of President Washington and President Lincoln, the symbols of the eagle, and the weird eye on top of the pyramid.

I'd forgotten about this money. Seeing it, something deep in me relaxes. One less thing now holds us back.

Mami stands and counts the money, her back straight. "Eighty-four dollars," she says. "I knew it was eighty-four."

Tati lays the money flat, then rolls it tightly and puts a rubber band around it. He puts it in his jacket pocket.

"You said we have no money," I say. "But we have this eighty-four dollars."

Tati sighs, saying, "That won't even get us out of Italy. Come with me to the car, Patrik."

We go down and out to the Fiat, now unhooked from the boat. Tati drives out of Trencin, past the spa.

Lines of cars are parked outside. Inside, people are steaming themselves in the big pools, drinking water from the springs of active volcanoes, lolling in the hot water.

"Can't we just leave tonight?" I ask Tati.

"We're not going to run like scared rabbits, Patrik."

"When *will* we leave?"

"Soon."

"But *Tati*!"

"No more, Patrik. I'm doing the best I can."

I press my forehead against the hard, cool window glass. I think of how, with the patrols on our tail, the rain will drop down in gray sheets. It will blow over all of us with great blinding sweeps. Only our orange life vests will be visible.

The car jerks as my father pulls off the road. He parks at a wooded spot where picnickers sometimes stop. Thankfully, we're alone.

"Keep watch, Patrik," he says.

Standing outside the car, I glance up and down the road. The pines sway, as if they, too, are keeping a lookout. Informants can come from any direction. They dig in the leaves for secrets.

With a screwdriver, Tati pries loose one corner of the door panel. Then he stuffs the American money—

I get a glimpse of the dull-green roll—deep into the body of the car.

When we get back, Mr. Holub is standing in the parking lot with his hands on his hips. A lit cigarette glows like the jewel of a fiery topaz.

He's been waiting for our return. He knows about the wad of dollars.

"Evening," Tati says, going straight up to him.

Mr. Holub is the one the trees look out for.

"Just come in from a drive?" Mr. Holub takes another cigarette from his pocket, lights it off the first one, and tosses the butt. He sounds friendly enough, natural enough.

I clench my fists in my pockets.

"Yes, Patrik and I were just . . ." Tati leans down to tie his shoe. "We went up to the castle to watch the sunset."

Mr. Holub nods, taking a long pull on the new cigarette. "Danika says you're going to Yugoslavia." He releases the smoke through his nose, then steps close to *The Fancy Free*. He wipes at the road dust with the flat of his hand.

"We are," I say firmly. "We're looking forward to testing out our boat."

Still amiable, Mr. Holub says, "This would be a good boat to leave with, Rumer." He crushes the butt of the first cigarette. "You know"—he narrows his eyes—"you could use a boat like this to get out of the country."

Tati musters a laugh. He slaps the boat. "Ha! Get out? Why would I want to do that? Where would I go?"

"Sometimes people have problems. . . ."

Tati and Mr. Holub lock gazes.

I head away from them. I head into the building, up the grimy stairwell, and into the apartment. Mami's nurse cap is hung on the peg, and I smell meat stew cooking.

In my room I listen for Tati's footsteps on the stairs. Maybe right now Mr. Holub is arresting him. I'm fretting and pacing when a note comes down on a string. I blink. But yes, it's a note. Is Danika about to apologize? Now, when it's too late? I open the window and pull in her message. I unfold the paper to read: *My father knows*.

Ice water slithers down my back. I run my finger over the words. This could be a trap. Yet I scrawl *Knows what?* I tie the note back onto the string and give a yank.

Right off, another note falls. The previous messages are scratched out and three new words are written very small: *That you're leaving.*

Again, a chill freezes my bones. I hear the front door open, then shut. *Should we stay?* I write. I hear Tati's voice. I jerk on the string.

A brand-new note drops. *Go!*

I write: *Thank you.*

I pace the room, waiting for more from Danika.

Out in the sea, suddenly all three patrols will turn around. But then a huge green blanket of a wave will sweep toward us. It'll crash over the boat, making the engine sputter. Leaving, it'll drag my envelope of photos and drawings into the sea. Everything will be gone. Danika. My entire old life.

The next wave may take our picnic. And the one after that will grab Bela's doll right out of her arms. Bela will throw up her breakfast into the bottom of the boat.

The rain will be falling more slowly by then. The sky will be lightening, so that I'll see my family instead of only their orange vests.

Suddenly, two objects will rise and fall in front of

the boat. Getting closer, we'll spot two people swimming way out there, two lucky ones who survived the storm without a boat.

It will be the woman who years ago swam out to sea with her child in an inner tube. We'll have found them at last.

The woman will call out, raising one arm.

We'll move the boat alongside. Tati will pull the child into the boat first, inner tube and all. The mother will climb in, causing the boat to tip sideways, taking on water. By then *The Fancy Free* will be riding dangerously low.

All of us will be shivering hard.

There's nothing more from Danika. I go to the kitchen, where Tati is standing close to Mami and her pot of stew. He has not been arrested after all. "Mr. Holub knows our plans," I say from the doorway.

Mami puts a finger to her lips and points to Bela, who is putting shoes on her doll.

Tati closes his eyes, squeezes them tight. Then he opens them again, saying, "I guessed as much."

"We have to get out of here," I say. "Now."

"How can we go if Mr. Holub knows?" Mami asks, her big spoon dripping gravy onto the floor.

"We'll have to try," Tati says. "We don't have any choice."

"We should leave tonight," I say.

"Impossible," says Tati.

"We could sneak away."

"Impossible," Tati repeats.

"Right away in the morning, then. We have to try."

Mami drops the spoon onto the kitchen table. She goes to Bela and takes her onto her lap. She brings yarn from her pocket and laces it over Bela's fingers, then begins to play a game of cat's cradle.

Tati casts a glance at Bela. "All right, then. Tomorrow we are going on vacation. In the meanwhile," he says, beginning to pace the length of the kitchen, "we'll act perfectly friendly toward the Holubs. As if nothing is wrong."

I go into the darkroom. I have no film to develop. I have nothing to do in here. I lock the door. The red light shines softly. The chemicals lie still in their baths.

We'll motor on, all of us drenched. We'll shudder with cold. The storm will have passed, but night will arrive. Once, we'll stop to pour gasoline from one of the red cans, and the stinking stuff will spill on my feet.

Lights

In the morning, I help Tati carry down the four suit-cases, the big canvas tent, and the sleeping bags. Tati even manages to whistle. Mami pushes a box of canned food into the hallway, saying, "Find a place for this in the boat. Food in Yugoslavia will be too expensive for us."

Hauling down the cans, I trip on the bottom step. When everything crashes to the floor, my legs fold under me and my knees bump onto the hard concrete. With my bones screaming, I want to lie here and never get up.

But I pick myself up off the steps, pack the crate, and go on.

When the car is full, I take a last stroll through our apartment. It looks as if we still lived here, as if we've truly just gone on a vacation. But really, everything is up for grabs. Someone will get Mami's silver candlesticks. Someone will get Tati's diploma and pretend to be a doctor. Someone will help himself to my darkroom chemicals and will develop the pictures I can't take.

When I go down the stairs for the last time, a small group of people has gathered, the early morning light yellowing their faces. There is Mr. and Mrs. Holub, along with Mami's friend Jarmila, from the fifth floor. No Danika. It's not a big send-off, since the official story is that we'll be back in two weeks. But if we do return, it'll be as captives. It won't be to these people, nor to the lives we live now.

Standing on the back staircase, still out of everyone's sight, I look for signs on Mr. Holub's face. Shifty eyes, an unconvincing smile. But he looks completely normal and is even helping Tati with the last bit of packing. I glance toward the big gate. I look for someone standing outside, ready to stop us. Someone with handcuffs. I examine the sky, where a helicopter might suddenly appear.

I hear footsteps. It's Danika coming down, wearing a green dress with daisies around the hem. Seeing her reddened eyes, I take a chance and hold out my arms.

She comes into those arms, sinking her weight against my chest.

My insides twist like wrung-out washing. Breathing in her mix of soap and honey, I grit my teeth against a stupid gush of tears. With words no louder than breath, I ask, "Are we going to make it, Danika? Are we going to get away?"

She gives the tiniest of shrugs, her shoulder blades moving under my hands.

Outside, Tati honks the horn.

"Time to go," I murmur.

She tilts back her head, squinting her lovely blue eyes, as if seeing me for the first time. "I'm sorry. So sorry . . . for everything."

"Me, too. I'm sorry, too."

"So we can be friends? In spite of it all?"

I only nod, not trusting my voice.

The horn sounds again, and the world tumbles back to me.

"Just a minute," she says. "Wait just a minute." Very solemnly, she pretends to hand me something. "Take this. Please take it."

I hold out my hand.

"It's your staff," she says.

I close my hand around the air, almost feeling the grain of the wood.

In an old familiar gesture, Danika reaches over me, saying, "Bend down a little." It's as if she's putting on a shirt. My magical one. She slips the magical belt around my waist, then stands back to announce: "Now you have the power to escape all traps."

"Oh, Danika . . ." I pretend to cinch the belt tighter.

She laughs a little at that and slips her hand into mine.

Together we walk into the morning, to where the blue Fiat, *The Fancy Free,* and my family await me.

In the backseat, Bela has already made a little nest for herself and her doll. Tati is double-checking the trailer hitch. Mami wipes tears with her sleeve.

I squeeze Danika's hand, squeeze again, then let go.

Tati climbs into the car and starts it up. I climb in, too, and shut the door. Danika is crying now. *Too openly,* I think. I blink hard, forcing back my own gush. While the little gathering stands waving, Tati backs up, aiming the Fiat toward the road. He angles it back and forth, the boat trailer thrashing like a caught fish.

Mami presses a handkerchief to her damp face.

Bela dances her doll at the window.

Finally we're on the road, lined up to go. No one has stopped us. No one has handcuffed or shackled us. Then, without warning, Bela calls out the window: "Good-bye forever, everyone!"

I knew it. I knew Bela would blab.

"Bela!" Tati exclaims. "You know it's not forever."

I study their faces. No change. None at all. They are all just waving.

I will be the first to see the lights of Italy. Twinkling like yellow stars, they'll drift behind shreds of cloud. The lights will grow bigger, brighter. I'll make out buildings, a pier extending into the water toward us.

Without hindrance, I'll steer *The Fancy Free* to the Italian pier, one step closer to the wondrous freedom of Scranton, Pennsylvania.

Now Mr. and Mrs. Holub and Jarmila give one last wave and turn away, moving toward the building. I catch a glimpse of Danika in her green dress.

As Tati turns the car, I get up on my knees. I thrust aside the camping gear, shoving it heedlessly, until the back window is clear.

With my camera that still has no film, I aim and focus, then push the silver button. I shoot one last beautiful photograph.

ACKNOWLEDGMENTS

I would like to acknowledge Milan Smolko, who escaped from Czechoslovakia as a teen and inspired this story; Mirek Sykora and Ann Brownlee Sykora, who assisted with anecdotes and cultural accuracy; my two critique groups—the Snail Society and the Flaming Tulips—for their careful reading and insights; Kelly Sonnack, my agent, who supported me throughout the process; and finally, my editor, Deborah Noyes Wayshak, for her unerring guidance and faith in me.